The Urbana Free Library

To renew: call 217-367-4057
or go to "*urbanafreelibrary.org*"
and select "Renew/Request Items"

Rise

L. Annette Binder

WINNER OF THE 2011 MARY MCCARTHY PRIZE IN SHORT FICTION
SELECTED BY LAURA KASISCHKE

Sarabande  Books

LOUISVILLE, KENTUCKY

FIRST EDITION

Managing Editor
Sarabande Books, Inc.
2234 Dundee Road, Suite 200
Louisville, KY 40205

Library of Congress Cataloging-in-Publication Data

Binder, L. Annette, 1967–
  Rise : stories / by L. Annette Binder ; foreword by Laura Kasischke.
     p. cm.
  "Winner of the 2011 Mary McCarthy Prize in short fiction."
  ISBN 978-1-936747-39-9 (pbk. : alk. paper)
  1. Fairy tales. I. Title.
  PS3602.I5245R57 2012
  813'.6—dc23
                          2011041615

Cover photograph: "Starlings" by Danny Green, an award-winning natural history photographer based in the UK. www.dannygreenphotography.com.

Cover and text design by Kirkby Gann Tittle.

Manufactured in Canada.
This book is printed on acid-free paper.

Sarabande Books is a nonprofit literary organization.

The Kentucky Arts Council, the state arts agency, supports Sarabande Books with state tax dollars and federal funding from the National Endowment for the Arts.

For my parents and for David and Georgia Lee

CONTENTS

ACKNOWLEDGMENTS

These stories, sometimes in slightly different form, appeared in the following publications:

One Story and *The Pushcart Prize XXXVI: Best of the Small Presses*: "Nephilim"
Third Coast: "Galatea"
Beloit Fiction Journal: "Nod"
Bellingham Review: "Wrecking Ball"
Short Story: "Shelter"
Quarterly West: "Tremble"
The Southern Review: "Dead Languages"
Crab Orchard Review: "Rise"
Green Mountains Review: "Halo"
American Short Fiction: "Sea of Tranquility"
Avery Anthology: "Weights and Measures"
Carve: "Mourning the Departed"
Indiana Review: "Sidewinder"
Fairy Tale Review: "Lay My Head"

Thank you to everyone who read these stories and helped me improve them:

My teachers Ron Carlson, Andrew Sean Greer, Christine Schutt, Jayne Lewis, and especially Michelle Latiolais.

The editors who published and helped improve these stories, especially Jeanne Leiby, Pei-Ling Lue, and Hannah Tinti.

John Reed and his band of midnight pirates.

My writer and reader friends—Raisa Tolchinsky, Karen Bryan, and Cat Robson.

Laura Kasischke, who saw something in these stories.

A million thanks to Sarah Gorham, Kirby Gann, Caroline Casey, and all the folks at Sarabande Books for their support of this book and for all the great work they do.

My father, Gerd, who shared with me his love of books and history, and my mother, Helena, who has told me since I was seven that I have a very good vocabulary. I could wish for no more loving and supportive parents.

And David Kahn, my favorite blacksmith, and our daughter, Georgia Lee—my two greatest blessings.

Foreword

It occurred to me, while reading L. Annette Binder's collection *Rise*, that perhaps the most magical skill a true storyteller possesses is the ability to restore to the reader the sense of what a strange voyage we're on, this life. It seems that this strangeness of life would be evident at all times, but the fact is that, except during moments of heightened awareness, the edges get dull, the awe boils down. Things are what they are, and they fail to astonish.

But, while reading *Rise*, each time I put it down, I found the colors brighter, the objects around me more intriguing, the dialogue overheard more full of portent, and the whole idea of *story*—how it can be both a craft and just the weirdness of *what happens*—more alive.

What a heroic feat!

L. Annette Binder has gone so deeply, and with such mystical brilliance and loyalty, into her own world that she has brought mine to me in high relief. Or, she has climbed a rickety ladder to get the view from up there in order to share it with me. Or, she has spent the night out in the orchard, listening in on what the worms in the apples have to say. Or, she has risked a fortune on a number, and, lucky for me, has won.

This feeling that she was helping me, via her stories, to *see* differently caused me to recall an anecdote told by the anthropologist Richard Grossinger in his book *The Night Sky*. He writes of an experience he had while doing research on people who believed they had been abducted by aliens:

> At a UFO meeeting that I attended in the basement of a bank in Hamtramck, Michigan, the gathering was told that it was honored by visitors from Venus and Saturn. I looked around the room, and suddenly everyone appeared strange and extraterrestrial. Everyone was a candidate.

There are moments like this in life—bright flashes of intensity. Some kind of defamiliarization has taken place. We see it all differently, however briefly. But there aren't very many of them. *Rise* reminds us that real storytellers exist to bring these experiences to us.

To everything she sets her fabulist eye on, L. Annette Binder brings this intensity. Like all of our best storytellers, she reacquaints us with our world. Borges would have recognized this genius, as would have Poe, O'Connor, and Mann. Like these writers (and others whose writing she recalls—Cormac McCarthy, Joan Didion, Steven Millhauser, the Brothers Grimm), L. Annette Binder brings word to us from beyond the quotidian of what is always there. She both casts a spell and breaks it. To experience *Rise* is as much to experience wonder (again, and as if for the first time) as it is to read a collection of wonderful stories.

RISE

Nephilim

Freda weighed eighteen pounds when she was born. Her feet were each six inches long. At ten she was taller than her father. Five foot eleven and one half inches standing in her socks. *I can't keep you in shoes,* her mother would say, and they went to Woolworth's for men's cloth slippers. Her mother cut them open up front to leave room for Freda's toes. She'd stitch flowers in the fabric to pretty up the seams, forget-me-nots and daisies and yellow bushel roses. *Some of your daddy's people are tall,* she'd say. *Your Aunt Mary had hands like a butcher. By God her grip was strong,* and they sat beside the radio while her mother worked the needle. They listened to *The Doctor's Wife* and *Tales of the Texas Rangers.*

Sometimes she felt her bones growing while she lay in bed. This was when the sensation was still new. Before it became as familiar as the pounding of her heart. The house was quiet except for the planes out by the base and Tishko behind the Weavers' house, who barked at the moon and stars. *That dog's got a streak in him,* Mr. Weaver always said. *I bet he's part wolf on his momma's side,* and Tishko was out there howling and the summer air was sweet and her bones were pushing their way outward. Stretching her from socket to socket. *There's nothing wrong with you,* her mother said. *You're pretty as a Gibson Girl. You just had your growth spurt early,* but Freda knew better. She knew it when she was only ten.

•

God was a blacksmith and her bones were the iron. He was drawing them out with the hammer. God was a spinner working the wheel and she was his silken thread. Seven foot even by the time she was sixteen and she knew all the names they called her. Tripod and eel and swizzle stick. Stork and bones and Merkel like the triple-jointed Ragdoll who fought against the Flash. Red for the redwoods out in California. Socket like a wrench and Malibu like the car, and she took those names. She held her book bag against her chest and took them as her own.

Her house had been her parents' house. They'd bought it new when Freda was nine. A split-level built in 1951 that cost seven thousand dollars even. She was thirty-seven now and sleeping in their bedroom. It had low ceilings and low doorways, and she knew all the places she needed to stoop. Every three weeks she cleaned the upstairs windows by standing on the lawn. She used a bucket with hot vinegar water, and she didn't mind the smell. There was a blue jay nest in the eaves up there, and they really fouled the panes.

"Lady what's your problem." A little boy was standing on the sidewalk with his bike. He had a shoe box strapped to the rack behind the seat. "I never saw a person big as you."

"These blue jays are my problem," she said. "Look at the mess they're making."

"I bet they got a nest up there. My momma says they're pests."

"Where's your house?"

"We're new," he said. He pointed four doors up to where the Clevelands used to live. "We're in the yellow house but my momma she's gonna paint it because it's much too bright. But she can't right now because of the fumes. In September I'm starting at the Bristol School. That's when I'm getting a brother."

"How do you know it won't be a girl?"

"No way," he said. "I asked my mom for a brother. And she can tell anyhow. She gets sick in the mornings and not at night and she says only boys do that. Sometimes she's in there for hours."

Freda set her bucket down and wiped her wet hands down the front of her pants. It was May, but the air still had some bite and this boy was wearing only a pair of thin cotton shorts. She pointed to the back of his bike. "What do you have in that box?"

"I'm looking for crickets," he said. "My lizard Freddy he's got a condition."

"I've got plenty of those," she said. "They're eating up my flowers." The waterlily tulips were done for the year, but her lady tulips were just getting started. They were red on the outside but their insides were yellow and orange and it was like having two different gardens when they finally opened.

"You got some nice ones," he said. "You got more than Mrs. Dillman and she's out there every day." He rubbed his thumb against his jaw like somebody much older. He was wearing a T-shirt from the Freedom Train. She could see it now that she was closer. She could see his collar bones and the hollow beneath his ribs and how his legs were knobby as drumsticks and brown already from the sun.

"You want to see those birds? You want to see the babies sitting in the nest?" She held out her arms, and he came to her. He should have been afraid, but he leaned his bike against her maple and walked across her lawn. She hoisted him upward and toward the eaves and he was all bones, this little boy. Her hands fit perfectly around his waist.

The nephilim were the children of fallen angels and ordinary women. Her mother had told her this years ago. Her mother who was so tiny when they laid her out because she shrank as she got older. *I'm five foot two and one half,* she always said, and she was angry if the doctors tried to round the number down, but she knew about the nephilim. She'd read about them in books. How they were giants on the earth before the coming of the floods and how they left their bones behind. That part wasn't in the Bible, but her mother said it was true. Enormous piles of bones and the sun bleached them and they turned to rock and that's why we have the mountains. *Look,* she'd say, *we can see them from our window,* and she'd point to Pikes Peak and it looked like skin, that mountain. Pink as skin when the sun hit it and not just piled-up bones.

•

His name was Teddy Fitz. His baby sister was born that September, and every morning he walked past Freda's house on his way to school. He didn't close his jacket, not even when the wind started to blow. He wore tennis shoes in the snow. She paid him five dollars to shovel her walk. She bought him knit caps at Walgreens and thick fleece gloves, and he looked so serious while he worked. She could see in his face the man he'd become, in the set of his jaw and how his eyes slanted downward.

Five dollars to shovel the walk and seven fifty when summer came because she couldn't push the mower. Another five to help with the bulbs the following September. She told him where to plant them so she wouldn't have to bend. Her knees were starting to go. Pretty soon she'd need a walker.

"This looks like an onion," he said, holding up one of the bulbs. "How's it gonna grow a flower?" He made holes with the dibber and set the bulbs inside and he was careful when he patted down the dirt so they wouldn't turn.

"Just wait," she said. "You'll see in April how it works." The plant was inside. It was only sleeping. It was waiting for springtime when the dirt would get warm.

He shook his head at the wheelbarrow she'd filled with bulbs. "You sure bought a lot. It'll take days to get these planted."

"I'll give you five dollars extra if you do them all today."

She sat in a mesh lawn chair and let him work. Her bones were burning again. She'd be on crutches in a few years, and the wheelchair would come next. Her internist Dr. Spielman was bringing up options at every visit. There was an operation they could try. He knew a pituitary specialist who'd had good luck with a patient in Tulsa, a man who was almost eight feet tall and the operation took out his tumor and stopped his bones from growing. Her tumor might be too big by now. Surgery might not be an option, but only the experts would know for sure. Her spine would begin to curve if they didn't do something. She'd get diabetes or high blood pressure, and eventually her heart would stop. The radiation therapy was better than it used to be. Surgeons were more precise now than they'd ever been before, and she needed to be brave.

She leaned back in her chair and watched this perfect boy. He held the bulbs like they were porcelain cups, and he gently laid them down. The wind was still warm when it blew and it ruffled up his blond hair. He wiped his forehead against the inside of his elbow, but he kept working because those five dollars were waiting and they'd bring him that much closer to the skateboard he wanted. She'd give him ten when he finished and not just five. She'd buy him the skateboard herself, but his mother wouldn't like it.

Anna Haining Bates was seven foot five and one half inches at her tallest. She died the day before she would have turned forty-two. Her heart stopped while she was sleeping. Jane Bunford was another giantess. She was perfectly normal until she was eleven and took a fall from her bike. She cracked her skull against the pavement and then she started growing. Things turn in an instant, this was the lesson. Hit your head and everything changes. The tallest man in modern days was Robert Pershing Wadlow. He was eight foot eleven inches just before he died, and when he was nine he carried his father up the stairs just to show he could. She knew this from the *Guinness Book of World Records*. She bought a new copy every year. How strange it would be to stand next to a man and to look him in the eye. To feel the smallness of her hands when he took them in his.

"My dad says I'm gonna be short like my mom." He sat on the bag of leaves like it was a beanbag chair. He sat right beside her and took a rest, and his nose was smudged from the dust. He'd filled five bags already just from the maple tree. "He says my sister will be taller than me when she's done growing."

Freda leaned across her mesh chair and wiped the smudge away with her thumb. "My momma was a tiny lady. Her waist was smaller than my neck." There's no knowing how things would go, she wanted to tell him. He could be a giant when he grew up. One day he might walk on the moon. She stroked his cheek with her thumb, too, but he shook himself free.

"What about your dad? He must have been pretty big."

"My dad was about as tall as yours. That just goes to show you. And how can your daddy know how big your sister'll be? She isn't even three."

"He says she's got those monkey arms."

"We're all monkeys," she said. "We all come from the same place."

"I'm no monkey." He shook his head. "Those are very dirty animals. I went to the Cheyenne Mountain Zoo last year and they were throwing poop." He got back up and finished her front yard and then started on the back. He fished the elm leaves out from her beds and all the ponderosa needles, and she followed him on her canes and stood there for a while. The canes were only temporary. Some days she didn't even need them. The canes were for when the pressure changed or when the winds started blowing. As soon as summer came, she'd walk without any problems. She just needed that dry air.

According to the Book of Enoch, the nephilim were three hundred cubits tall. Four hundred fifty feet, give or take. That's three times higher than the Holly Sugar Building on Cascade, which was only fourteen stories. They were bigger than Barkayal and Samyaza and Akibeel and all their angel fathers, and they were always hungry. Nothing could fill them up. Not the birds or the fish or the grains in the fields, not the sand snakes or the lizards. They stripped the forests and ate the bark from the trees. They turned against ordinary men when the last food was gone. They went after the newborn babies.

Teddy bought himself a skateboard with some of the money he'd earned. A cheap one from Target and then a nicer one from the Acme Pawnshop down on Fountain. He bought himself a bike, too. One of those Speedsters and the paint was gray and dull from the sun, but he waxed it anyway. *Just wait till I'm old enough to get my learner's permit,* he'd say. *I've already got six hundred and thirty-four dollars,* and his car fund was growing every day. His parents shouted almost every evening. Freda could hear them four doors down. Sometimes his mother went away for a few days at a time, and Teddy never said anything about it, not even when Freda asked.

He delivered the *Gazette* in the morning and for a while he delivered the *Sun*, too. That was back in the late 1970s when the Springs still had two daily papers. He threw the papers from his bike without even slowing down. He knew just how to toss them so they landed on people's front steps and not in their flower beds. She waited sometimes to see him go by. She stood behind her screen door, and he cycled past with an athlete's grace. What was it like to move like that, to never be still and never be tired? He stood on his pedals and pumped them hard, and the other boys were so ordinary compared to him.

The Lord ordered Michael and Raphael to kill the nephilim one by one. To bind their fathers under the hills for seventy generations. The crops could grow once they were gone. The trees could push out shoots. Hunger is a terrible thing, her mother had told her more than once. It's like a hot rock in your belly and you can feel it burning. She knew this from her childhood in Nebraska. The days so black you couldn't find your way from the steps to your front door. The wind blew the seeds right off the field, and days later the alfalfa sprouted in barnyards and distant cemeteries where the seeds had scattered. Hunger has no mercy when it comes, she'd say. But hunger was their burden, and they should have carried it.

He bought Mrs. Dillman's old '72 Gremlin the week he turned sixteen. It was butterscotch gold with racing stripes, and he waved at Freda when he drove by. His arm hung out the window, and he was proud as Hannibal coming over the Alps the way he raised his hand. He used cloth diapers and three coats of Mothers Wax to bring out the luster. He installed a fancy K&N air filter, and every day after school he was out there in the driveway. He rolled back and forth under the car, and his sister stood beside him and handed him the wrenches.

That's where he was the day his mother left. Freda saw the truck when it pulled up. Teddy brought the suitcases out to the curb and hoisted them into the bed, and he held the door for his mother. He didn't cry and he didn't wave when the truck rounded the corner. He kept on waxing his car. So many coats Freda lost count, and he was still there working the diaper when the sky was dark and the driveway floodlights came on. His mother had a boyfriend and his mother was gone, and Teddy was still there working when Freda went to bed.

He painted her trim the summer before his senior year. He sanded her gutters, too, and painted them chocolate brown. He cut down a broken branch from her maple tree and brushed sealant on the open bark to keep the fungus out. She looked for jobs to give him because next summer he'd be gone. He was a cadet in the Junior ROTC, and he'd be going away to college. Up to Boulder or Greeley or maybe to Fort Collins. He did pushups and jumping jacks on his front lawn, and once his sister sat sidesaddle along his back to make the pushups harder.

He sealed the cracks in her driveway and painted her cement steps. All she could do was watch. She leaned on her walker like it was a banister and told him what to do. The juniper bushes needed trimming and some of her window well covers were cracked, and after he was done the house looked as nice as it did when her parents were alive and still working in the garden.

She kept her household money in a Folgers Coffee can. He came inside with her and poured himself a lemonade from her pitcher while she counted out the bills. Somewhere up the street there were children shouting and the sounds of splashing water. Mrs. Dillman had an above-ground pool she filled every summer for her grandkids. Freda took ten five-dollar bills and set them on the table. Her walker scraped across the linoleum as she pulled it around. The kitchen felt so big when he was there beside her.

"I think the rubber's loose." He pointed to the bottom of her walker. "I can glue it back on for you and then it'll be real smooth." He leaned in to get a better look, and Freda caught his chin and cupped it in her hand. That face she'd known since he was little. That sad face and those eyes that slanted downward. She wanted to remember him. He wasn't even gone yet. He was right here in her kitchen, but she was seeing him from some distant point ten or twenty years in the future. She was seeing him in her memory standing by her table. He was seventeen and in a dirty white T-shirt and his skin was pink from the sun.

In her memory she kissed him. His lips tasted like lemons. In her memory he didn't pull away. She felt so small there beside him, small as a girl when he touched her cheek. His hands were callused from the shears, and all her life she'd never know anything more perfect than his breath against her skin.

Her mother said a heart at peace gives life to the body. Also, we are all small in the eyes of the Lord. Don't listen when they call you names. How could they know what it's like? She heard her mother's voice those nights when the air was still. Those summer nights when she could feel her jawbone growing. She was almost fifty and the radiation wasn't working anymore. Her teeth were starting to spread, and her features were getting coarser. She didn't look in the mirror when she washed her face. She closed her eyes, but she could feel the ridge across her forehead where the skin had started to thicken. Her mother's voice came back to her after all these years. *Don't be afraid*, she said. *He raises us upward. He carries us inside His palm*, and sometimes Freda could feel her mother's fingers press against her cheek.

He took a pretty girl to the prom. But you already knew that's how things would go. He took a pretty girl with tiny wrists and ankles, and there were more until he found the girl who was meant for him. She wasn't the prettiest in the group, but she looked like him, how her eyes slanted. She was a good three inches taller than him even in her Converse sneakers. She wore his denim jacket and his plaid flannel shirts and he opened the car door for her and closed it again, and they drove together like they'd always been a pair.

Somebody tied her feet to the ground and her hands to the wooden wheel. Somebody else worked the wheel and pulled her upward, stretching all the muscles around her sockets. It was her companion, this feeling. She couldn't call it pain. It was the pulling she felt in her bones. Sometimes it carried her upward, and she knew her mother was right. Sometimes it pulled her the other way. She moved

downward through the dirt where her flowers had once grown, down
to the rocks that would become the mountains, and she was so small
beside them.

All beautiful things go away. Everyone knows this is true. Their son
looked like him, and he rode a bike just like him, too. They were back
for the first time in years. They came to check on Grandpa Fitz. They
weeded his rock beds and adjusted the sprinklers, and Teddy's wife
was out there in her capris, trimming back the hedges. Freda rolled
closer to the window so she could see them better. That boy with eyes
like his daddy and those skinny brown legs. His hair almost white
from the sun. Every year it would get a little darker. And her Teddy
was out there cutting the elm tree back from the power lines. His son
ran circles around him and pointed to the sky, and he didn't listen
when Teddy shouted. His momma had to pull him away from the
falling branches. Teddy was almost thirty. How could that be. He
was a first lieutenant. She knew this from Mrs. Dillman's youngest
daughter. In another few years he'd be a captain because anything was
possible in this world. He sat up there in the branches, and his back
was so straight.

He came by in the evening with a jelly jar full of flowers.
Snapdragons and tiger lilies and snowfire roses. His wife had put ice
cubes in the water to keep the blossoms fresh. Teddy knocked on
her door, and when she didn't answer he knocked a little louder. She
could see him from the window in her living room. He was standing
on the wheelchair ramp, and his boy was there beside him. He waited
a good five minutes before he set the jar outside her door. He wouldn't
have said anything about her jawbone or her bent fingers or how her
back was shaped like an S. He would have taken her hand and knelt
down to greet her, but she stayed in her spot by the window. His face
was like a mirror, and it was better not to look.

Galatea

She used arnica and bromelain to minimize the swelling. Vitamin K and quercetin and silicone dressings. As soon as she'd healed from one procedure she went back for another. The doctors tightened up her neck by cutting downward through her chin. They cut her eyelids, too, and they used thread to lift the muscles in her cheeks. It was strong as fishing line, and sometimes she felt it above her jaw. This tiny filament that kept her face from falling. Every month there were advances. Lasers to burn away spider veins and brown spots and injectable filler. She wanted all these things. She lurked on message boards, and the women there talked like lovers about their surgeons. She wrote down all the names.

Her mother said she was starting to look a little Slavic. She stood at the stove with a wooden spoon. "It's not natural what you're doing," she said. "Just look how your eyes are slanting." Her mother's face was spotted from all those years in the garden. She hadn't worn a sunhat back then because nobody did, and she didn't wear one now because what did it matter. She was almost eighty, and her hair was white around her face and soft as cotton balls. You were a good girl growing up, Carol. That's what she always said. Don't make me worry now.

They sat together when the eggs were ready. Carol went to visit every Sunday. She wore sunglasses because her eyes were still sore from the needle. The doctor had massaged the droplets once they were inside. He kneaded her skin like dough. She told her mother about the new doctors up in Denver. They had offices in Aspen and California, too. They were always taking planes. "They're the best in the country," she said. The light was starting to come through the café curtains, and they were the same ones from when Carol was in college more than thirty years before. The sun had bleached them a paler yellow. The Little Red Riding Hood cookie jar was the same, too, and the refrigerator magnets with faded columbines. A picture of Jenny from the second grade. Her hair was tied up in ribbons. She looked just like Carol had when Carol was a girl. "They specialize in veins."

"You could see the pyramids if you wanted or those volcanoes in Hawaii." Her mother stirred Splenda into her coffee. Her hands were spotted just like her cheeks. They were speckled as robin eggs.

"They worked on Sharon Stone."

"Can't you take your glasses off? I can hardly see your face."

Carol shook her head. The sun was really shining now. Another windy December day, and she didn't want to squint. The room smelled of coffee and eggs overcooked in butter. Her mother always overheated the frying pan because eggs carry diseases. Five hundred people a year died from salmonella, and probably more the news won't tell us. Her mother knew the numbers. She spent hours on WebMD.

"Someday they won't need scalpels. They'll go straight to the genes."

"God help us then," her mother said, and she took the remote from the table. It was almost nine o'clock, and she never missed Dr. Dyer. He talked about how the spirit is all around us, how it fills us from inside and we can find it if we look.

Carol pushed her plate away before it was empty. Aging was a disease, and they were working on a cure. There were entire villages in Japan where people lived to a hundred and twenty. All they ate was fish. "Those scientists at Berkeley were just on TV again. If we starve ourselves we can live forever. That's what they were saying."

"None of it will bring them back." Her mother shifted in her chair. She winced a little because her right hip was bad. The socket was starting to fail. "Be grateful for what you have." She raised the remote like a wand and aimed it over Carol's shoulder.

•

Stop the clocks and turn them back. Stop the changing of the seasons. Another gray winter and her girl was gone. Another muddy spring. Change the bulbs from white to pink. Use dark shades to diffuse the light. She learned about lighting from the boards and her rejuvenation magazines. Candlelight was gentlest of all, and she had scented pillars on all her tables. The apartment was hushed as a church when she lit them at night. It was sweet with the smell of roses.

The specialist in Denver looked at her hands. He held them in his and raised them up to the light. The veins looked so blue, and Carol felt ashamed. They rose like rivers beneath her skin. There were ads on the walls for eyelash conditioners and Juvéderm, and the women in the posters were perfect. They were brown and ivory and gold, and they looked past the camera when they smiled. They had no pores and no wrinkles, no dark spots from the sun. Their whole lives they'd never know the touch of unkind hands.

The doctors were using Radiesse at the clinic. Just a few injections along the bones where the skin had gotten thin. The veins were trickier, but endoscopic lasers helped. They used a wire thin as any filament and it burns them from inside. She knew these things. She had her list of questions ready.

The doctor in charge was named Mittelman. He was probably fifty, but his hair was still dark. He looked like a character from *Days of Our Lives*. "It's hereditary," he said. "Some people just have thin skin." He pressed his fingers against her veins, and the residents leaned in to see. They were so serious with their clipboards, and one of them was a girl in high-top tennis shoes. A medical student who wasn't older than twenty-six. They might have been classmates once, Jenny and this girl. They might have known each other as children.

Mittelman looked right at Carol when he talked. His eyes were pale in the light from the window, and she wondered what he saw. The surgeries she'd had, the lasers and the doctors with their needles. Surgeons were like artists and like painters. They knew each other's work.

"Come closer," he said, and he motioned toward the residents. They gathered around, those young heads, and Carol felt a tightness in her chest. Her eyes began to brim. Who could say why the tears came. There wasn't any logical reason. She thought of Jenny and her gray eyes. Pale as sea glass and fringed with those dark lashes. There was a terrible silence in the room. The doctor stepped back and the residents looked down at their notebooks, and Jenny was alive in another place. Maybe she lived in Boulder. That's where the young people went. There were coffeehouses on every corner.

"I'm doing this for myself," Carol said. She wiped her wet cheeks with her palms. She knew the things she had to say. The surgery wouldn't change her life. She had realistic expectations. "It's for my birthday. It's a gift I'm getting for myself." She said these things, and the doctor saw right through them.

She'd let go of her baby's hand. It was only for a minute. Four days until Christmas. The mall was crowded with crying babies and mothers pushing strollers. People didn't apologize if they hit you with their bags. She let go of her baby's hand and looked for her car keys. She reached inside her purse, and her Bic pen had broken and the ink was puddled at the bottom. It was leaking through the leather. She knew the moments now. She knew them all as if they were showing on some white screen, and she watched them as they happened. She looked over her shoulder and a little boy was screaming in the aisle. His eyes were squeezed shut, and he clenched his fists like somebody having a seizure. He'd be twenty-two now, maybe twenty-three. He'd be graduating from college. His mother was on her knees trying to calm him down. People fussed with their bags and their winter coats, and her baby wasn't there. "Jenny," she said, and her voice was shrill. "Jenny, come here." She turned in circles, and she saw a half dozen little girls, but none of them wore a red jumper. They didn't have ribbons in their hair.

The security guards came first and then four policemen who'd been eating at Wendy's. They smelled like onions from their burgers. The policemen and the fire truck and her husband who drove straight from his office at the Schlage Lock company. They walked through the mall, endless loops around the food court, and Santa was there with all the little kids waiting in line. Around the parking lot and up Chelton where the snow was melting beside the curbs. Up and down the streets and back to the mall where the stores were closing for the evening and all the stars came out and they didn't sleep that night or the next. The hours stretched and contracted and time stopped without her baby. The sun didn't rise or set.

Three days later or maybe it was a week, and her fingers were black from the ink. She scrubbed until her skin was raw. Until Rick took away the scouring pads. "What are you doing," he said. "You're bleeding on the rug." She kept washing because her hands were never clean. Lava Soap and Comet couldn't take away the stain.

The bosses were in a meeting. She made sure they had their coffee and their French crullers. Mr. Fitz the owner was picky about his donuts. What would we do without you, he told her more than once. You keep this office running. She was a bookkeeper and not a secretary, but she didn't mind the work. Marnelle the secretary was out on maternity leave. Last month she had twin baby girls, and Carol had the place to herself. She watered the ferns and cleaned the betta fish bowl because the water always got cloudy.

Fitz looked contented when he came out of the conference room. His shirt strained around his belly. "By God you're a hard worker," he said. "That look of concentration." He stopped in front of Carol's bay and rapped his knuckles on the counter. He was losing all his hair. He was the grandson of the original owners. It was Fitzes all the way up the company tree. Concrete runs in our veins, he'd say. That's why we're all so heavy. He laughed each time he said it, as if the joke were new.

She waited until he was inside his office. He had golf balls in plexiglass domes from every course he'd ever played and pictures of his chubby daughters. Mahogany furniture and green felt coasters and a miniature Mount Rushmore cast in cement. The door closed and his chair creaked when he sat down, and that's when she turned to the accounts.

She took only what she needed. Almost every month she wrote a few checks to herself. It wasn't hard because she knew the requirements for setting up small businesses. She named them JB Holdings and JB Services and JLB Supplies, and she set up accounts at the Exchange National Bank and the Ent Credit Union on Wahsatch. She had so many accounts and so many names, and she tracked them all on spreadsheets. She paid her taxes, too, because that's how they got Capone. He shot people with his Tommy gun, but they nailed him on his returns. She set up those accounts and made out the checks, and she should have felt bad when Mr. Fitz worked so hard to keep the family business going. He didn't complain when she took vacation time or left early for her appointments. She was a thief, and she should have been ashamed.

Mr. Fitz was getting angry behind his door. His voice always changed when he called the guys at the plant. The kiln was down again, and it would be another week before they got the coils. "Sweet Jesus," he said. "Can't you do it right for once? Can't you take care of a single goddamn thing?" His chair rolled across the plastic mat that protected his green carpet. She could hear the wheels going back and forth, and his face was probably pink by now. He'd be in there for hours.

Carol finished all the checks before he was done with the call. He was really yelling now. Someday he'd have a seizure if he wasn't careful. Someday his heart would stop. She signed the checks and set them in envelopes. She took the real ones to the mailbox, and then she went back to the message boards and looked for some new names.

Dr. Ashrawi mapped all the places for the needles. His eyes were the color of walnuts, and they looked serious even when he smiled. He had done his training in Beirut. Women came to see him from Cairo and the Gulf, and he was only in Denver for the winter. He was teaching at the DU Medical School. He catered to the ladies in Cherry Creek who were tired of their hands. Whose skin was dried as jerky from all their tennis games.

"Relax, Ms. Bishop," he said. "Listen to the music." This was the moment. It was always the moment when the world narrowed to a point. She knew the sting when it came. She knew the needle and the burning. This is what it feels like when there's a fire in your veins. The walls were gray like her baby's eyes. There were lilies on the counter. She could smell them from her chair. That sweet smell and the cleaners, too, and gentle music through the speakers. "Lucy in the Sky with Diamonds." "Light My Fire." Just the melody and no words. Rick had loved the Doors. He'd danced to them when they first bought the house. There was no furniture in the living room, not even a pillow or a rug, only the Sansui quadraphonic system in the middle of the room. He turned the volume on high because that's what people did when they had no neighbors through the walls. He slid along the floor in his wool camping socks. *We're home*, he said. *Every brick belongs to us.* He swung his arms around, and there was nothing graceful in how he moved and that was why she loved him.

The Nagys came and the Biedelmanns and all the neighbor boys. They made a fan and walked the fields behind the Emerson Middle School. Rick led them like a captain, Rick who had two teenagers now and lived up in Fort Collins. He drew circles on the map, and the circles kept getting wider. The police came with their dogs and volunteers on horses, and nobody found a trace. The Christmas trees came down and her baby was gone. In April the tulips broke through. She kept the hairs from Jenny's bristle brush. She kept the dirty laundry and the bed just as it was. She'd pestered Jenny to make her own bed. *You're almost seven*, she'd said. *You need to learn to clean your room*, and now she left it messy. She was grateful for the clutter and the marker scribbles on the wall. Grateful for the chipped baseboards because these were the things her girl had touched.

The dishes stayed in the washer for weeks. It was hard to turn the dial to make it run. The leaves weren't raked and the bills went unpaid and it was hard to remember what day it was or why they were together. She saw Jenny everywhere she looked. She'd tell Rick to stop the car, to turn, to look where she was pointing. A girl walking in the mall who tilts her head the way she used to. A mother pushing a stroller. She looked for Jenny in every mother's face and in every nursing baby. In all the fields outside of town where they were building those new houses. Especially in the fields because that's where she was sleeping.

You've got to stop, Rick used to say. *It's not healthy what you're doing.* He gripped the steering wheel until his knuckles were white, and he didn't slow down to look, not even when she cried.

She stopped by the old house. She went there after every procedure. Her hands were wrapped up tight, but she could bend her fingers. Five couples since she'd sold it and at least two single mothers. Eleven children between them, and this new couple was the worst. Look at the weeds in the gravel bed and how the trim was peeling. The garbage can was tipped sideways on the curb, and that was where it stayed. She parked across the street and watched the kids play in the yard. A fat little girl and her blond brother. The mother didn't watch them the way she should. They chased each other up and down the sidewalk, and she needed to be more careful.

She opened the car windows because it was getting warm. She leaned back in her seat, and she felt the blood beating in her hands. It hurt more than the other procedures, even more than when they lifted her jaw and set the hooks behind her ears. It hurt and the sky was clear and how many hours had she spent in that yard planting bulbs with Jenny. How many summer afternoons running through the sprinklers. The first lilies were blooming on the corner where old Mrs. Lucas used to live. She worked the beds every day and that was where they found her. The neighborhood was the same, one brick rancher after the next, but the city was growing around it. All those new wood houses with their pastel colors and dirty asphalt shingles. They spread over the fields where the cottonwood trees used to flower. Every day the concrete mixers drove up and down Academy. They poured the slabs in the empty fields and the city unfolded itself like a map. It pressed against the mountains. The concrete covered all the places Jenny had ever been and the place where she might be.

She was having a bad reaction. Two weeks of swelling, and her hands were wrapped in gauze because she didn't want to see them. Two weeks of dropping the phone and fumbling with the doorknobs. Her mother came and washed her laundry. She brought lentil soup and garlic mashed potatoes.

"I just don't understand you," her mother told her. "I don't think I ever will."

They ate together on the sofa, and Carol dropped her spoon. She picked it up and wiped it on her shirt, and her mother shook her head. "You can't go on like this," her mother said. "You're oranger than a pumpkin."

Carol blew over the surface of the soup the way she used to when she was little.

Her mother was wrong. She could go on like this forever. "You oversalted it this time," Carol said. "Or maybe it's the ham."

Her mother did the dishes. She ran the vacuum, too, and mopped the bathroom tiles. "Quit punishing yourself," her mother said. She knelt in the shower stall, and Carol felt ashamed to see her mother working the brush. Her hip had gotten worse. The doctors were saying it was time to get a new one, but her mother said it was a racket. Those joints were probably made in China and they'd break easier than bones. They'd chip like teacups. She cleaned the shower and scrubbed the toilet bowl because it was getting a ring, and Carol stood beside the bucket with her bandaged hands.

"They found that girl in Littleton," Carol said. Twenty years in a garden shed, and the police brought her back home. She was alive and her baby was, too, and time had stopped for her while she was gone. She came out, and the world was changed. Who knew if she recognized her mother's face.

"They need to leave those folks alone." Her mother pushed herself up, and her hip cracked just like a shot. "Always following them around with cameras." She started in about the cemetery again. How Carol should go visit. It was healthier than watching all those crime shows. It didn't matter if the grave was empty. People didn't go to the cemetery to visit the dead. They went to visit their memories. She talked to Herman every week there and told him about his girl. How she was a bookkeeper and how she'd worked her way through college.

Her mother rested on the sofa when she was done cleaning. She propped up her hips with cushions. Carol sat beside her, and the light was gentle in the room. "He'd be proud of you," her mother said. She stroked the hair from Carol's eyes. "He always said you were good with numbers." She held Carol's hands, but gently, gently. She pressed them against her heart.

The blood came back once the swelling had subsided. It found its way to another vein, and that vein broke through the surface. She went to see Dr. Ashrawi as soon as she saw the bulge inside her skin. "That can happen," the doctor said. "I see it in twenty percent of patients." He looked at her right hand because it was worse than her left. He held it like a suitor asking her to dance.

He talked about other options and diminishing returns. They could try sclerotherapy. Just a couple of injections and the vein seals shut. It turns into a scar beneath the skin. There could be cramps after the treatments and a few broken blood vessels. "The results are typically good," the doctor said. "But there are no guarantees." His voice was deep and wavered a little, and she wondered what he sounded like when he spoke his native language. It was probably sunny in Lebanon. The women were all beautiful, and the air smelled sweet from the oranges.

Sclerotherapy or maybe vein removal. They could cut them out, all of them, and her hands would be smooth, but then she'd have some scarring and pain from the stitches. The doctor talked and he looked only at her for those few minutes. The world slowed, and the phones went quiet in the hall. It was just the two of them and nobody else, not even his pretty receptionist who looked like one of the ladies in the brochures. Her perfect oval of a face and skin that never saw the sun. Her mother talked about Dr. Dyer and finding your way forward, but the answers were all right here. In this quiet office where the ladies sat in plush chairs and waited for their consultations. Vases with orchids submerged in water and soft music coming through the speakers and she'd stay here all day if she could. This doctor would help her and if he changed his mind, she would find another and another. She had a high pain threshold. She never felt a thing.

She wrapped her hands when she got to the car. She didn't want to see them. She should clean her apartment and pay her bills and wash her dirty Jetta. All these things, and she drove instead. It was

April, and in another month her girl would be twenty-nine. Whole satellite cities had grown up north. More people were coming from California, and pretty soon there'd be no place to put them. Down the freeway and off at Academy and back to the old neighborhood. Past the old house and the medical buildings where the Kmart used to be. Past the Printers Home and up the winding street and through those iron gates. Of all the empty fields in the city this is the one where she knew she wouldn't find her girl.

Paradiso, Himalayan Black. Indian Aurora. The stones came from India and Greece. The sun warmed them when it shined. She touched them as she walked the rows. She'd picked the prettiest one. She'd spent hours with the brochures. The grass was wet from the sprinklers, and her boot heels sank into the muddy patches. Let it be warm where her baby was. Her baby whose hands were always cold. Who needed the heavy blanket even in summer. She slept like an Egyptian with her arms folded across her chest. All that granite and the winters didn't touch it. Not the April sun.

She read the names and the dates, and they all had lived longer than her Jenny. One woman two rows over was born in 1897 and Jenny was lost before her. Soon there'd be no one who would remember her. Her grandma would die and Carol, too, and Jenny would die with them. She had no brothers or sisters. Every person who walks the earth leaves behind a mark. Her mother said this, and maybe she believed it. But what mark could Jenny leave when she was only seven? Her classmates were parents now and her teachers were all retired, and nobody would remember her in another thirty years. No one would say her name.

She pressed her hands together. The blood comes back when you're living. It always finds its way. The city was pulsing around her. The cars drove by so fast just outside the gates. The Cinema 70 was a Kawasaki dealership now. The movies they'd watched together, and all those velvet seats were gone. Sirens sounded from the fire station down on Circle, and she felt her heart beating. Her mother was almost eighty, and her grandmother had been ninety-four when she passed. The women in her family lived to an old old age.

She sat down on a bench across from Jenny's marker. It was noon and the sun was shining, and one of the maple trees was early and coming into bud. Conjure the memories. Bring them to the surface. This was the city where her girl was born. Her name was Jennifer Lee Bishop. She was a second grader at the Monroe School and she swung on the monkey bars. Her hair flew upward in a tangle. It smelled like berries from her shampoo. They went to Fargo's for their pizzas and the numbers appeared in the mirror. Skating at the Broadmoor rink before they tore it down and Jenny had bumped into Scotty Hamilton there once and spilled Pepsi on his jacket. She never watched where she was going. Both her front teeth were chipped. This was the city and these were the things her girl had touched, and she looked at her wrapped hands.

Nod

By the third night he was certain he'd never sleep again. She lay there breathing just inches from his side. She pulled the blanket away from him and turned toward the wall, and the dogs in the alley were barking again. He listened to them and waited for the sun to rise, and he wasn't entirely awake and he wasn't sleeping either. He was deep inside that fog. Three days it had followed him to work. It hazed his vision and nothing helped, not the treadmill and not the energy drinks he'd started buying. He'd never liked coffee or soda pop, and now he was drinking things that tasted like chemicals and burning hair. He couldn't focus anymore. The spreadsheets all looked the same. He'd sit at the keyboard and try to clear his eyes, but the clouds stayed even after the second can.

He went out to the living room and turned on the TV. Today they were hunting black bears. Somewhere in central Oregon. He watched his shows every day. They were recording while he worked. They'd be waiting for him when he got home, and it didn't matter if Becky complained. He'd watch them anyway. Accounting theory and business law couldn't compete with survivalists who ate lichen and those guys in Idaho who'd stalked an elk for days. They were wild-eyed when they came back across the ice. They looked like visiting prophets.

The sky was always gray in Oregon. This was how it seemed. A gentle drizzle was always coming down, and the hunters went along the clearcuts and fields of blackened trees. The bears liked the damp ground where the huckleberries grew. They liked abandoned orchards and acorns from the tanoak trees. Another month and they'd be sleeping. All that work overturning logs and looking for grubs, finding the last of the berries and fallen fruit, and they'd sleep it off. If they weren't fat enough by November, they'd die in their dens. He closed his eyes and lay back against the chair. He covered his legs with the chenille throw.

She'd started talking about his birthday this week. She loved having something to plan. *It's coming up*, she'd say. *It's just around the corner. What do you think about Toscanini's? They do a nice job with the platters.*

She meant well, but all her talk about parties just made him nervous. Forty-three wasn't a big year. There wasn't any reason to celebrate, and she went on and on. She was thinking of a carrot cake and bottles of the house merlot, and was there anyone from work he'd like to invite. There was space for twenty in the big room, maybe twenty-five. She was sweet the way she smiled. Her front teeth overlapped a little, and her hair never stayed the way it should, and all these things she hated were the ones that he loved best. He should go back to bed. He should lie down beside her and pull her against his belly, but he stayed in front of the TV. He lay there, and it pushed down on him. The weight of all that air. He felt it and he closed his eyes, but he didn't fall asleep.

The city was its own wilderness. It was wild like the forest or the mountaintops, and they'd need equipment to survive. Last August a transformer blew on the corner, and the power crew didn't come when he called. No electricity for three days, and by the end the apartment smelled like garbage and sweaty socks. All their food went bad, and they had to toss the top tier of their wedding cake she'd been saving for years. That was when he started with the catalogues. Really started. He applied for a Cabela's charge card. He bought hand-crank radios and water purifiers and bear spray because it was on sale. The gear outgrew the hallway closet. Boxes sat on the kitchen table and behind the bedroom door, and Becky wasn't happy. He'd started watching his shows in a camping chair, and she looked lonely on the sofa. Sometimes she even cried. *I got you one, too,* he told her. *Look how nice it is. It has these cup holders on each side,* but she looked at the piles and the new Pertex sleeping bags and stayed just where she was.

Four days without sleep. Four days and his eyes were gritty. It hurt to blink, and his throat had that metallic feel. His boss Marshall was waiting for him to finish the boxes. Thirty-six boxes still needed coding, and the interns in the conference room looked lost behind the papers. Marshall wasn't happy. *Fish,* he said, *you're taking too long. You're making it much too hard.* And what good did it do to explain, when Marshall hadn't done any real work in years. It takes time to build a database and to review all those company files. Time to find the things that matter, and Marshall didn't understand. He sat behind his desk surrounded by pictures of his cranky children and a wife with beetle eyes. All around him people were moving rocks. That's how Fish thought of it, moving rocks across a field from one end to the other. He sweated and worked and carried those rocks, and there were always more. They grew and multiplied.

Snake boots were on sale. Upland vests and blizzard hoods, he marked these down for later. He wanted cold-weather gear. It wasn't even the middle of October, and the peaks were already white. Every time the catalogues came he found more things he needed. He tabbed them like college textbooks, and he tried to ignore her when she came into the kitchen. She was watching over his shoulder again. She was waiting for him to finish. She opened the fridge and looked inside. She opened it a half dozen times a day, but she usually shut it without taking anything out. She was on Weight Watchers again and careful with her points.

She took a diet Sprite and popped it open. "Maybe your mom can come." She sat down beside him. "I think she's in town this year. Her cruise isn't till December." She tucked a curl behind her ear. She was always careful when she brought up his mother. He could see how she hesitated, unsure of what she'd find when she pulled that curtain back.

"Sure," he said. He closed one catalogue and reached for another. "She'd love to see you."

"Now you're just being sour. You're always happy afterward. It's only before when you make a fuss."

She took out her planner and wrote down some more names. Things were coming together. She'd ordered a cake from the new bakery down on Platte, and she could tell him the flavors but not the decorations because those were a surprise. Even Marshall was coming, she said. It wouldn't be right to invite the associates and the interns and not to invite the boss. He looked up from the catalogue then because she didn't know. She lived with him in this tiny place, this third-floor apartment with its sloping floors, and they were mysteries one to the other.

His father died at forty-three. Peacefully, in his sleep. That's what people said. They told him to be thankful because at least his daddy didn't suffer. There're worse ways to go, they'd say. Car accidents and dismemberments and serial killers, fires and creeping disease. Better to close your eyes and not open them again. That's the way for me. They were wrong, of course. They had no idea. Even two doors down he could hear the gasps and that strange rattle. His father's heart must have been thrashing behind his ribs. It was struggling to break free.

The ambulance came with all its sirens going. *Get back to bed*, his mother shouted when she saw him standing by the door. *Get back inside your room.* Her eyes were bright and hard, and she frightened him more than his father, who lay unmoving on the bed. He saw the shadows of the paramedics beneath his door, walking in thick rubber boots because it was raining outside. It was coming down strong and steady. He heard them yell and one of the vases broke in the hall, and his mother wasn't crying anymore. She wasn't talking at all. They left together, his mother and the paramedics and his father on a stretcher. In her panic she'd forgotten him, her only child who wasn't even eight. She left him alone inside the house. The ambulance didn't run its sirens when it pulled away. It went slowly in the rain, and that was when he knew. He stayed in his room until she came back. He waited beneath his blankets.

Five days, six days, seven, eight. He slept an hour or two at most. He slept and woke, and the neighbors were arguing. They slammed their cupboard doors, and the wife was crying. Cars drove by with their radios too loud. Power ballads and Johnny Cash and rappers he didn't know. The sounds came through the floorboards and the cracks around the window air conditioner. They filled the room, and Becky sighed sometimes, but she didn't wake. She was talking to the people inside her dreams. Her voice was gentle. She sounded like a mother talking to her baby.

It wasn't good all his reading about night diseases. He surfed the Web too much looking for symptoms. Bangungot in the Philippines and the Japanese called it pokkuri and there were more names for it, this strange disease that killed young men in their sleep. People over there blamed the angry spirits. A fat ghost lady of the forest who sat across men's chests and kept their hearts from beating. An old man who smothered their faces out of spite. It was easy to laugh at those explanations, but in the end they were as good as any. What could science say, what comfort could it give when sometimes a heart just stops? It stops at night when you're forty-three and your wife is sleeping beside you. When your son is two doors down in his Spiderman pajamas. It stops, and staying awake wasn't the answer either. What about fatal insomnia, now there was a disease. It killed those Italian families by keeping them awake. Strange curling proteins tangled up their brains, and maybe that's why Becky was sleeping and he was listening to cars. She turned and threw her arm across his chest, and she opened her lips the way babies do.

Sonata, Ambien, Lunesta, Ativan, Becky knew all the names. She knew people who slept the whole night through with only a single pill at bedtime. *Make an appointment with Doctor Tischmann,* she told him. *Go see him for a prescription. Maybe it's your thyroid. You ought to have it checked.* She bought him melatonin drops in the meanwhile. Chamomile and kava kava and strange little scented pouches. Lemon balm and lavender and Saint-John's-wort and other witchy things. She set them on his nightstand, and that was where he left them.

They had the party the Saturday before his birthday. She'd hired mariachis to play even though Toscanini's was an Italian restaurant and people were eating pasta. The band strolled around in their charro suits and sashes, and even he had to laugh when his mother set down her beaded purse and danced with one of the interns. And he'd never have guessed old Marshall would be out there in the middle. He was flapping his arms like a German at an Oktoberfest. He was doing the chicken dance. *It's a great party, Fish,* he was saying from across the floor. His face was pink, and there were sweat marks beneath his arms. *Your wife is really a prize.*

Fish moved away from the group. He had a piece of cake, and it was frosted in a camo pattern. She'd chosen Mossy Oak, and there were plastic bears on top and little men with guns. She'd given him a certificate for wing-shooting classes. He'd have an instructor who'd show him how to mount a gun and how to follow the clays. *What's the point of watching all those shows,* she'd wanted to know. *What's the point if you've never even held a gun?* Sporting clays were okay, but she didn't want him to kill birds. He could tell it made her sad to think of them falling in midflight. She liked a steak every now and then, but at heart she was a vegetarian.

He finished his cake and used his fork to scrape the last of the frosting from the plate. Becky and his mother were standing beside the platters. His mother was talking. Becky tilted her head the way she did when she was really paying attention. She was looking over at him, and even from across the room he saw something in her face. Disappointment maybe or surprise.

It was strange seeing them together. Becky who was older now than his mother had been that night. How young she'd been and he didn't notice. A widow at thirty-four. All those years and she hadn't remarried. Clyde the banker and old Jerry the retired school principal and Daniel the rare gun dealer who wore a turquoise bolo and more that he couldn't remember. She was nice to them one after the next. She invited them in for drinks but turned down all their offers.

His mother came over just as he set down his plate. Her hands were shaking from the wine. They'd be shakier still before the party was over. *It can't be right*, she said. *My boy is forty-three. You're making me feel old.* She reached for him. She pulled him close, and she felt light in his arms. Tiny as a bird that was only hollow bones and feathers.

He saw angels in the streets. Gold-colored birds flew upward into the branches, and everywhere there was a pattern to things. Old women were beautiful with their shopping bags. They were beautiful how they closed their collars against the chill. The sky was clear because the wind was blowing hard, and the sun shone, but it gave no warmth. He needed to close his eyes. He needed to rest before he could walk again, but he kept going because he was late and Marshall would be waiting. He passed the old Antlers Hotel and then the Holly Sugar Building, and there were men up high on a tiny platform washing down the windows. A girl walked in front of him. She was wearing a down vest. The wind caught her ponytail and blew it upward like a fan. He caught a glimpse of her face reflected in the window, and she was another angel. He wanted to fall to his knees.

There were patterns in the shadows of the branches. In the starlings that flew and the spreadsheets, especially the spreadsheets. The numbers were their own language, and he spent hours watching them move. He kept his wool coat on because it was cold inside the office. He shivered at his keyboard. He trembled and laughed, and the tears rolled down his cheeks. Marshall came and stood beside his bay. He looked a little worried. Sweet Marshall with his moon face. Fish laughed even harder. He held his stomach and set his head between his knees the way passengers are supposed to when their plane is about to crash.

She was waiting for him by the door. Marshall must have called her. She took his coat and his laptop bag and set them on the coffee table.

"You need to go to the doctor. We've waited long enough."

"Tomorrow," he said. "Tomorrow I'll go." He really would. Tomorrow was his birthday, and he'd call at least and make an appointment. That's what he told her, but he didn't know if it was true. He said it without thinking. His voice didn't sound like his own.

She relaxed a little. She turned on his shows and set the table in front of the TV and not in the kitchen where they usually ate. He took his plate to his camping chair, and she didn't grumble for once. She tucked her feet beneath her and ate on the sofa, picking at her chicken and the broccoli florets. She rubbed his shoulders when he finished. She really took her time. *I can feel the tension*, she was saying. *Right here in your neck.* He shivered under her fingers. He felt it all the way down his arms, and it was how his mother had touched him the morning she came back. She'd held him by the scruff, as if he were a kitten. His father was dead, and all the softness was gone from her face.

Becky left the dishes in the sink and came with him to bed. She'd cleaned out the bedroom. The bicycle was gone and all her nursing books. The laundry was sorted and the hampers were closed, and there were new shades on the windows. She'd bought vinyl black-out shades and screwed them into the frames herself. She'd gotten the holes off center on one of them, and he felt a surge of gratitude when he saw how it hung crooked. His eyes welled up, and he didn't know why.

She waited until his spot was warm, and then she moved in close. "I'll stay awake until you sleep. We'll stay awake together."

The artists on the second floor were having another party. A woman was shouting over the music. *I knew it*, she said. *I knew it all along.* Something broke, glass shattered, and people clapped and laughed. He met them sometimes on the stairs, his neighbors, and they never said hello. He was invisible to them. He was just another pale guy in a suit. They wore their youth like armor.

He rolled onto his back, but he didn't let go of her hand. They'd gone to the badlands once together. In her peacock blue Chevy Cavalier. They took the trip right after she'd finished nursing school. He'd dropped out of law school and was waiting for the next thing, and it was the last time they'd both be free. He didn't know it then, of course. Back then he didn't know much except that he loved her. Ten days driving the desert up through Nevada and Utah and back into Colorado. They stopped at the Green River and looked at the dinosaur bones. At night they rolled the windows down and opened up the sunroof. There were no lights anywhere, no cars and no people and nothing outside but rocks and the wheeling stars.

Her breathing was deep and steady, but she was still squeezing his hand. She was telling him she was awake. He squeezed it back. The rocks had looked like shipwrecks in places. It hurt to look at the sky. They'd stood together by the bank and watched that slow green water. He'd wanted to buy a canoe right then and follow where it went. Even now he felt its pull.

The party downstairs was winding down. The music stopped midsong, and the door opened and closed and opened again. The guests were laughing as they went down the stairs. They talked in loud drunken voices. He should have told her. She shouldn't have to hear things from his mother. He squeezed her hand again. He closed his eyes and waited.

Wrecking Ball

First he drilled out the top of the cartridge. It was one of the empties from his dad's old BB gun. He opened up the shotgun shells next and gathered up their powder. His friend Bean had given him four shells. Bean who was scared to hold a gun even though his daddy was a soldier. He tamped the powder into the cartridge and dropped the BB in. Bean leaned in close to watch. *Let me clamp it*, Bean was saying. *I know how to do it, Mason. I know it well as you.* He crowded in beside the vice, but Mason ignored him because he didn't have a gentle touch with the metal. It needed only a little bend, just enough to keep the BB in once the powder had ignited.

Bean took the cartridge when Mason was done. He had the match heads ready. He stuffed them down the canister's neck, working them in tight. He stuck his tongue out the way he did when he was taking a test. Mason stepped back and let him work. The fuse was easy. Not even Bean could mess it up. Bean tore the filter off one of the Marlboros that lay on the workbench. He stuck the cigarette in the hole so the tobacco touched the match heads.

It was dark outside though it wasn't even five. Dark as January and just about as cold. People stayed inside this time of year. They sat on their sofas and watched their shows, and their living room windows glowed blue. Mason went first, and Bean followed in his yellow parka. *Idiot*, Mason said. *Take it off and leave it.* Wearing colors instead of black. What good were those grades Bean got, what good all his science experiments, if he had no sense when it mattered. Mason pointed at the parka, and Bean took it off and went outside in his camo shirt.

They walked along the street, their heads low because the wind was blowing. "My fingers are stiff already," Bean was saying. "I need to go to Miami. I'm gonna go to South Beach and look at the Brazilian girls."

"Miami, Ohio maybe." Mason held the canister against his parka. He cradled it in his hand. "Next year you'll be at Loaf 'n Jug if you're lucky. You'll be wiping down the windows for those Seventh-day Adventists."

Bean laughed at that. He knew his shortcomings, even Mason had to agree. He wasn't afraid to look stupid. They came up to old Foster's metal mailbox. It was the nicest mailbox on the street. It had two wooden blue jays perched on top and lilac branches painted down the sides. It was like everything else at the Foster house. Immaculate and a little fussy.

Mason gave the canister to Bean, who held it like a chalice. Mason took a breath and looked along the street to make sure nobody was turning at the corner. His hand shook when he flicked the lighter. Bean started fidgeting. He was shivering from the wind. "Hold still," Mason said. "Quit your shaking before I burn you by mistake," but his hands shook a little, too.

They tried to act casual once the bomb was inside. They tried to move slowly, but they ended up running anyway. They ran, the both of them, they ran with their arms pumping, and they slipped along the ice where old Mrs. Fieberling always forgot to shovel. Who knew skinny Bean could move like that. He was fast as Mason who could have been on track, that's what the coach said. *If only you'd apply yourself.* They reached Bean's old Camry at the same time and knelt down against the tires. Mason closed his eyes. He covered his mouth and waited. The air was so cold it burnt going down. So cold he felt his nose hairs freeze, and he was just where he wanted to be.

The cigarette was burning in the mailbox. That perfect orange circle was coming closer to the hole. The cigarette would light the match heads, and the powder would ignite. All that pressure inside and nowhere to go. Nowhere because the neck was bent and the BB was blocking the way. His hands were numb, and he rubbed them together. He cracked his knuckles in turn. This was only the beginning. He'd find a bigger canister. He'd get more shells and empty out the powder.

Twelve minutes in and Bean shook him by the shoulder. "It should have gone by now." He pointed to his watch. His voice went up high as a girl's.

"Maybe it's taking a little longer. Maybe it's the cold."

"I knew this was a bad idea," Bean said. "I knew we'd mess this up." He clenched and unclenched his fists. He was talking about how it was a crime to mess with mailboxes. It was a federal offense.

"That's for U.S. mailboxes, imbecile. Not Foster's painted birds."

Bean stood up. "I'm going to get it. I'll take it out before anybody sees."

"Don't be stupid." Mason grabbed Bean by the elbow.

"I knew this was a bad idea," Bean said again. He shook himself free and stepped away from the car.

Bean walked slowly this time. He didn't listen when Mason called. He walked instead like it was summertime, and he latched his thumbs in his front jean pockets. His arms were skinny as knitting needles. They looked almost blue in the light. He went past Mrs. Fieberling's house, and Mason stood up to watch. The streetlights were coming on, first on Pikes Peak Avenue and then along the side streets. They shone over the snowbanks and the cars. Bean stopped just before the Foster house. He wasn't twenty feet from the box. The wind had stopped blowing and the stars were out, and Mason felt it before it happened. He felt it through the stillness and the beating of his heart. The flame was coming to the powder. It was quiet in the street. Peaceful how it must have been right before the stars were born. He held his arms out the way conductors do. All the windows shook in the houses as if responding to his signal. They rattled in their aluminum frames, and a smoke ball rose over the mailbox. It made a perfect mushroom cloud.

Bean went to his knees like somebody who saw Jesus. He covered both his ears. Mason stayed where he was, and things moved slowly around him. Those painted birds flew over the street. They were bent at strange angles. The mailbox looked like a porcupine from all the metal pieces that had blasted their way out. It leaned over on its base, and Foster was opening his front door. He was wearing a plaid bathrobe and his mouth was open wide, but Mason didn't care. He saw only how beautiful things were. How the smoke drifted upward, how it was white against the sky and it wasn't even done yet and he was thinking about the next one. He'd use a bigger cartridge. He'd find some sprinkler pipe.

One hundred fifty hours sweeping the streets. Picking up garbage from the interstate. People dropped diapers along the shoulder and scuffed up tennis shoes. They left crates behind and headless Barbie dolls and broken TV sets. Mason gathered them up and bagged them. He walked through the weeds, and all he thought about was a piece of pipe.

Bean wasn't the same, not even after the bones in his ears had healed. He talked about his body and how it was a vessel. There was a city by the river, and the river was of gold. They cleaned roads together on Thursdays. They filled up their bags, and Mason asked him for more shells. *Just a few*, he said, *just to tide me over*, but Bean shook his head. God had saved him for a reason, Bean said. It was time to set his face like flint. He had no need for shells anymore. He wanted no more fires.

Mason's mother wore amethyst and smoky quartz to help her concentration. Sometimes if he had a cough she set a rutilated crystal beside his bed. *It's as good as Robitussin*, she'd say. *It'll clear up all your passages.* She believed in chakras and Chinese herbs and the healing powers of talk therapy. Another three credits and she'd have her counseling degree.

She had a talk with him right after the sentencing. She talked about his needs and how she was here to help and not to judge because she'd made plenty of her own mistakes. She sat at the foot of his bed and sandwiched his hand between hers. "You were trying to tell me something," she said. "I should have listened more." She smiled a little, but her face was serious the way it used to be in church. She hugged him, and he pulled away and that was how it went.

•

The rocket club met on Thursdays in the soccer field behind the school. Sometimes he watched them from the bleachers. They used model rockets mostly, with single-use motors no bigger than a G. No metal parts and no liquid fuel and they had less than 125 grams of propellant. And still it was something when the rockets lifted. They made a beautiful ripping sound. Mr. Duffy the physics teacher ran between the launch pads. He was checking all the igniters and the fins. He waved to Mason and when Mason didn't come, he waved again and waited. His sweatshirt was tight across his belly. It said, "No Smoking. Unless you're on fire."

"Get over here," he said. "You can't see from where you are. You have to be real close." He set his hands on his hips and squinted, and his hair stuck to his forehead in wisps.

Mason stood beside him and watched some sophomores get their rocket ready. Theirs was bigger than the others, and they worked around it like surgeons. Three boys and a girl in overalls, but even through the loose bib he could see the outline of her breasts. The kids were kneeling around the pad and checking the fit of the airframe against the lugs. The rocket was painted red and it said "Copperhead" along the side. "Theirs is special," Duffy was saying. "They made it all by hand. They'll go to nationals with that one. They'll take an egg up 750 feet and bring it back unbroken." He left Mason and went over to the three kids to see about the switch.

Everybody stepped behind the orange cones that marked the safety zone. They shaded their eyes and waited. The sky was clear, but the wind was blowing from the mountains. He should have brought a jacket. He stood with the others and watched Duffy fuss with the solenoid switch. The taller boy had his arm around the girl's waist. He pulled her close, and she leaned her head against his shoulder. Her hair looked like copper in the sun.

Duffy started the countdown at ten instead of five. He shouted out the numbers, and everybody shouted with him. Mason joined in without meaning to. The air smelled sweet like chemicals and burning paper, and the rocket tore upward when they reached one. It was perfect the way stingrays are, perfect like eagles and diamondback snakes. It moved toward the sky with a predator's grace.

They caught the rocket when it floated back down. It barely

missed some trees. The red-haired girl came running. She held it high like a trophy. "Look at that," she said. "Look how sweet she landed." She was talking about the bulkhead and the o-rings in the chamber, but Mason wasn't listening. Who cared if the chute deployed or if the rocket made it back. It was the fire that mattered. It was the propellant and the blast and that sweet white chemical smoke. It was better than the black cats he'd shot off last July with Bean, better even than the canister that blew up Foster's mailbox.

Duffy came back to where Mason was standing. He was drinking coffee from a dented thermos. "Don't be so shy," he said. "We could use another set of hands." He gave Mason a serious look. "I've got a monster in my garage. You should come and see. The next one will be liquid fuel. Kerosene and liquid oxygen and there's nothing that kicks better."

He dreamt of perchlorate and igniters. He dreamt of Caroline's red hair. That was her name, that girl in the overalls. She took all the advanced classes. He was in remedial geometry and she was taking trig already and she'd be in college math by the time she was a senior. She was perfect how she laughed and how she held her books. The light followed her across every room. When she left she took it with her.

He wanted a lathe and a KitchenAid mixer. A small oven to bake propellant discs. He posted diagrams on his bedroom wall and lists of binders and bonding agents. He collected articles for Duffy, who listened carefully when he talked. For the first time he paid attention in chemistry class. He didn't doodle or look around the room. He worked at his computer every night and downloaded propellant handbooks. He heated up soup and Tater Tots so he could eat at his desk.

All the equations and the variables and it came down to a simple thing. It came down to the pressure inside the chamber. Give it an opening and you've got thrust. It will lift you if you let it. It will take you over the fields and the old brick school and the elm trees on Cascade that were dying from Chinese beetles. Those GoFast guys in

Denver sent their rocket up 77 miles. That was fifteen more than they needed to set the record. The distance to outer space was the same as the distance to Denver, 62 miles give or take. How strange to think about things that way. It wasn't really that far. With enough power things could break free from the curve of the earth. They wouldn't feel its pull. Pressure is all they needed. Pressure and an outlet, and now he had them both.

They took Route 24 to the wheat fields just past Calhan. Six of them in Duffy's old jeep and the sun shone in their eyes the whole way out. Everything looked rusty. The cars and the dirt and the storage sheds in the fields. As if the earth itself were made of iron and the ore was bleeding its way out.

There were at least a hundred people gathered in the field. They came in trucks and motor homes, and there was a school bus from a district out in Limon. Fathers stood with their sons, and everyone wore hand-printed name tags with rockets on them. Duffy's rocket was the star here. People pointed and gathered around the platform. With its five engines it weighed almost two hundred pounds. It looked like a half-scale patriot missile.

A father brought his son up close and lifted him higher so he could see. "That's a beauty," he said. "That one there can go up a mile." The boy smiled at that and the father swung him round, and Mason wanted to follow them. His father had lifted him like that once. They'd gone together to the fair and watched the rodeo cowboys. The air had been sweet with the smell of kettle corn and manure. Everything was touched with grace that day, and that's how today was, too. He wanted to slow things down. He wanted them to linger. The volcanic rumble of the rockets lifting and their trailing chemical vapors and Caroline who was pink from the sun. She was standing beneath the canopy with her hands behind her back.

Duffy's rocket went up almost eight thousand feet. Straight as an arrow shot from a bow. Mason felt the force of it through his sneakers. As if it were something living and not just cardboard and PVC. Duffy walked through the field like a conquering soldier. He ate sunflower seeds from a bag and spit them back out, and people came from all around to congratulate him. Somebody from the Western Rocketry newsletter interviewed him and took pictures of him with all his students. Five guys and Caroline at the center, Caroline who tilted her head at the camera and smiled.

They drove back together, sunburnt and laughing. Duffy dropped them off at his house, and they went home in their own cars, except for Mason who had walked. Duffy gave him a ride home. The house was dark because his mother was finishing up her last practicum so she could graduate in May. Some nights she didn't get home until eleven. Duffy set his hand on Mason's shoulder. "You were great today," he said. "You really helped me out." He leaned in close, so close that Mason could smell the coffee on his breath and the salt from the sunflower seeds.

There are so many ways a chamber can fail. This is what he learned from all his reading. The burn time can be too long, and the metal will start to erode. The nozzle bolts can fail or the weld up by the payload. Tiny cracks can form in the grain or air pockets that will increase the surface area of the burn. Flaws so small you'd need a microscope to see them, but the pressure inside will find them. It will always work its way out.

They'd gone together to spread the ashes up near the Continental Divide. She wore her hair loose because that was how his father had liked it. His father had been Mason and his grandfather, too. Three Mason Rigbys and two of them were dead. She played Elvis Costello and the Stones and all the others they'd listened to when they were young. *I can feel him*, she said. *I feel his spirit in the car*, and his plastic urn was strapped in the back seat like it was a baby. Mason looked out the window at the elm trees coming into bud. He didn't want to turn back and catch a glimpse of his father. It wasn't right to burn him, to turn him into powder. He knew this right away. What if the resurrection day came and everybody else rose up from their graves.

She said an Ojibwa prayer at the spot they picked. She talked about a Great Spirit and she could hear His voice and there were lessons to learn in every leaf and rock and tree. Mason didn't cry when they opened the urn. He waited for the wind. His father passed from his hand to the air and down the empty bluffs. Gone to powder as if he'd never been. Gone to the hillsides where there weren't any trees. No trees or flowers or fishing ponds. The wind carried him and the snows would cover him and he was going to the Atlantic now and the Pacific, too, because the Divide was the place where all the waters branched.

Duffy's basement had a wet bar and a dart board and a pool table with serious water damage. "I'll get around to fixing it," Duffy said. "It's somewhere on my list." His wife never came down there, so it belonged to him. It was better than a clubhouse. The other boys came sometimes, too, and they sat around the low table and watched movies and footage of other launches. Just before the end of the spring semester he gave them beer to celebrate. He swore them to keep it secret. "I drank when I was your age," he said. "It didn't hurt me any." There was a shine in his eyes. They looked warm as honey in the light.

Mason stayed after all the others had left. He didn't want to go home, and he didn't want to stay. He leaned back against the cushions, and Duffy brought out a stack of rocketry magazines. *Rockets* and *Extreme Rocketry* and *Sport Rocketry* and *Launch*. Some went back to the '90s. "You can borrow some if you like," he said. He spread them on the table, and there was a magazine with naked women, too. Its cover was creased, and the girl on the cover sat like an Indian with her legs open wide.

Duffy sat down beside him. "You can borrow that one, too." He reached for it and opened it and laid it across Mason's lap. He moved closer so he could turn the pages. He ran his finger along Mason's cheek, and Mason knew that feeling when it came. He knew it and closed his eyes. The wind was blowing again. It was turning things to powder.

Something was unfolding inside his chest. Every day he felt it growing. It expanded like a balloon and squeezed against his ribs. It was alive. Alive and mechanical, and it took away his air. He stood in the middle of the hallway. The others went around him. A few of them were running. They were laughing and swinging their books because the semester was almost over and the air outside was warm. At some point things went quiet and the classroom doors all closed. The teachers were reviewing their lesson plans. They were prepping the students for final exams, but Mason didn't go to his class, not even when the late bell rang. He walked through the front doors instead and down the concrete steps. The igniter wasn't ready yet. It was almost summer, and he had to finish it.

There was a reason his father had walked to lunch that day and a reason he crossed against the light. His mother said things were meant to be. They were printed on us before we were born. She seemed happy when she said it, as if it were a comfort. She talked about life plans and reincarnation and how it was better not to wonder why.

She was wrong, of course. There were always reasons, even if nobody ever saw them. The city bus had come too fast for a reason and the ambulance had been delayed, and sometime soon Duffy's rocket would launch before he was ready. He'd be hooking up the alligator clips. He'd be standing right there, and the exhaust would hit his skin. It would be hard afterward to figure out what happened. People might wonder if Duffy got sloppy with the wires. They'd ask about the e-match. Did he use a low current igniter by mistake? The continuity circuit could set it off if he did. It was just a little thing. Just a light bulb in the series, but with the wrong igniter it would be enough. They'd inspect the wreckage and look for reasons and miss the one that mattered.

He didn't go the next time they went to Calhan to shoot off Duffy's rocket. He stayed with his mother who was finally getting her degree. She was having a party and two dozen of her classmates were there, and they were therapists, all of them. Therapists married to more therapists. They sat on pillows and talked about processing things and progressive muscular relaxation. They looked serious when they talked about relaxing. There were cakes on the table and homemade sugar cookies, and his mother smiled when she cut the shortcake and passed the plates around. *Five years,* she was saying, *I can't believe how fast they went,* and her face was shiny. She winked at Mason the way she did when he was little. *And look how big my baby is. Next year he'll be a junior.*

It was hot outside. Three o'clock in the afternoon and not a cloud above the mountains. Mason stood alone by the window, and Foster was out there washing his old Lincoln. He wore rubber gloves and garden shoes. He worked the hose, and the droplets shone in the sun. In a little while Duffy would be setting up the rocket. The others would be back behind the cones. That's where he made them go, where he always made them go because he didn't joke about safety.

He could call Caroline and tell her to check the igniter. There was still a little time. He could call Duffy who carried his cell phone in a holster, but he drank his lemonade instead and stayed beside the window. *Get a little closer,* somebody said. *I need you guys to lean.* A group of graduates was standing with their diplomas. His mother's was framed already, and she held it against her chest as if it were a shield. All the books she read and all the seminars, and she didn't understand. Things happen for a reason, sure, but we make the reasons ourselves.

His mother came and stood beside him after the picture was done. She set her hands around his waist, and they looked together out the window. Foster walked down his driveway and rinsed off his new mailbox. It was shaped like a fire truck with a ladder and a hose. He dried it when he was done and made sure the latch was shut.

"I'm proud of you," she said. "All the work you're doing." She squeezed his waist, but he didn't turn around. He was a head taller than she was. Taller than his father had been, and he wasn't done growing.

They'd gone fishing once at the Eleven Mile Reservoir. They sat together on the rocks even after the wind picked up and churned the gray waters. The first drops fell, and the other people were packing up their gear. *The fish don't know it's raining,* his father said. *To them it's all the same.* They stayed until the sun went down. Until it was cold enough to need a jacket. His father smoked on the drive home. The tip of the cigarette was a perfect orange circle, and Mason fell asleep in the car. His father carried him inside.

The photographer came up to them. "Turn around, you two," he said. "This'll be a good one." He had one of those expensive digital cameras with a stabilizing lens.

They moved from the window to the entryway where the light was better. His mother leaned into him for the picture. Mason looked past the camera, past the deli platters and the people holding mimosas and Bloody Marys. He could feel it in his chest again. It was working its way out. He wanted things to stop, and he wanted them to burn. He wanted his father back from the mountains. The flash was dazzling when it went off. It lit up the whole room.

Shelter

He ignored their cats and how they stalked his fish pond and fouled his tomato beds. He ignored their music, too, and the sounds of breaking bottles. He tried to be neighborly. They didn't water the grass. They left their snowmobiles out the whole year long, and he said hello anyway. He left bags of tomatoes on their steps. Sometimes in winter he ran his blower up their walk because they were lazy when it came to shoveling. The husband Travis was built like a little fireplug and he wasn't more than forty, but he didn't bestir himself. Not even on his days off. The wife either, though she was home all day. And then in March they bought that fishing boat and parked it a foot over his property line. He didn't say anything that first afternoon or the next day. He was hoping it was only a temporary spot. But when they set down cinderblocks to keep the trailer from rolling, he steeled himself.

He asked Helen to watch for the truck. He was at the back pond when she called. He was checking the water levels. In winter he needed a trough heater to keep things moving, and they wouldn't eat much until the weather turned. But in summer they gathered around when he came. They ate what he threw down, the floating protein pellets and sometimes peas and watermelon and soft butter lettuce. "Frank," Helen said, "get on up here. You better hurry if you want to catch him." He hoisted up his work pants and went out front. He pretended to check on the mail though it wasn't even nine yet in the morning.

"Morning, Travis," he said. He shaded his eyes and looked up at the sky. "Looks like another beauty. It feels like May already."

Travis pulled his cooler and his toolbox out from the passenger side. "Don't much matter to me," he said. "Now that they got me working nights."

"It's no good those hours," Frank agreed. "They mess with your rhythms." He pointed to the boat. "That's a nice one. I saw her yesterday before you covered her up." He tried not to look at the black cigarette butts thrown across the dirt where the Fishers' lawn used to be. When he wasn't sleeping, Travis had one of those clove cigarettes in his hand, and Helen had to shut all the windows to keep out the spicy smell.

Travis was up on the steps. He was reaching for the door. "My cousin couldn't keep it. He plays the slots too much up in Cripple Creek."

Frank set his hand on the tarp that covered the boat. It was torn already and much too thin. A good hailstorm and it would be nothing but shreds. "Say, Travis," he said. "I was wondering if you could move her a little. She's over my property line." He pointed to the spot.

"Janel," Travis said. He pounded on the door. "I told you not to lock it. Get over here, you stupid bitch. Don't make me find my keys."

"It's not more than a foot. And I can help you if you want. I'll be around tonight."

Travis turned around and looked at him. "What's that you're saying?"

"It's just a foot or maybe two. But still."

Travis came over to where Frank was standing. He crouched and looked up and down the property line, from the sidewalk to the twin backyard gates. Frank's was freshly painted, and theirs was rotted through.

"You can tell from the tiger lilies coming up," Frank said. "They're on my side."

Travis shook his head. "That's my property." He smiled a little, and his teeth were brown from the cigarettes.

"We planted them thirty years ago and every year they bloom."

"I don't care who planted them," Travis said. He stood back up and looked at Frank, and his eyes were flat as aluminum.

Travis went back to his door. He reached for the knob. It was unlocked now, and his wife was watching from the window. When she saw Frank looking she let the curtain drop.

"It's not right," Frank said. "It's like stealing is what it is." The city would know. They had all the measurements in their books. He'd call them, and they'd come and see his house and how nice he kept it. It had a deck and a sprinkler system, and just last year he set pavers down by the vegetable garden. They'd see his house and all its improvements, and the line was clear where his property ended and theirs began. Even those lazy inspectors would have to agree. "You're stealing from us and all we've ever been was nice."

Travis didn't answer. He just picked his cooler and toolbox back up and went inside his house.

They lived for twenty or thirty years or even longer. Always swimming, always moving down in that dark water. He gave them names like Molly and Julius, and he knew them from their markings. Every spring he flushed the pumps and cleaned out the rotten watercress and added salt to the water and baking soda. He set down new lilies and sweet flag and floating heart and hyacinth, and for a little while before the algae bloomed the water was clear like gin.

He was knee-deep already, and this year he could feel the dampness in his bones. The fish moved all around him. Bright as copper pennies. They swam between his legs and bumped against his arms and flashed in the sunlight before diving back down. He counted them, and they were all there. They were starting to move fast again because the pond was 52 degrees already and getting warmer every day. He dropped in lava rock and some oyster shell to harden up the water.

One of the Fishers' cats hopped down from the fence. It came close to the pond. It watched him, and it wasn't scared, not even when he hissed. He leaned down. He cupped his hands in the water and splashed it. The cat ran then. It hid behind the purple plum tree and waited for him to leave. "Get going," he said. "Get back where you belong."

He put the new floss together and turned the pump back on, and once it got going he sat on the bench by the water's edge. He listened to its low mechanical hum. The forsythia was blooming and the tulips had sprouted early, and his son would be here with him, if he'd lived. He'd be married by now, but he'd come back and help them every spring. He closed his eyes. On days like this he almost believed their boy was alive. That he hadn't stopped kicking in his eighth month. That he'd been born at St. Francis Hospital and he'd grown up tall and the sun was shining now on both their heads. He set his hands together and spoke to his boy and called him by his name.

He tried the wife next, but she just held her arms across her chest. *I'm sorry, Mr. Muller,* was what she said. *He'll park it where he wants it.* The wind blew her thin blond hair back from her face, and she looked old as a grandma though she couldn't be more than thirty. She went inside when he started again. She pulled down the shades on every window that faced his house, and he knew it wasn't any use. That's when he went to the lumberyard and bought himself some posts.

He waited until Travis was at his shift, and then he dug the holes. He'd build the fence right through the boat if he could. He'd split that boat down the middle. But he did the next best thing. He set the first post right behind the trailer and the last one where his backyard fence began. That way everybody could see how the Fishers had crossed onto his land. He stretched a line between the posts and marked where the middle ones would be. It was hard to drive the hole digger into that winter dirt. It wouldn't get soft again until May. He struggled and cursed, and Helen brought him coffee when he called. She came out and shook her head. "You're making trouble again," she said. "Building a halfway fence. People will think we ran out of money." He waved her down and kept working, and his ribs were sore from opening the digger and pulling it back out.

The second night he put the middle posts in, burying them almost halfway into the ground. He packed them down with dirt instead of concrete and tamped them hard to keep them stable. He capped them when he was done so the rain wouldn't rot them. This fence needed to last. He used mortise joints to set the rails. Helen came out near the end and helped him nail the pickets. "I've been meaning to put up a fence," he told her. "It's been on my list for years."

She shook her head at that. "You've never talked about another fence before. You know it well as I do." She brushed down his jacket when he was done. She washed off his work shoes, and for once she didn't smile while she worked. Her face was puckered up tight.

Travis didn't come home until eight the next morning. Frank stood with his coffee cup at the living room window and watched him park his truck, in the driveway this time and not across the lawn. Travis didn't go straight inside. He went to his boat instead and looked at the finished fence. He tossed his cigarette butt down and ground it with his heel, and he reached inside his pocket for another. He looked at their window as if he could see through the curtains and into their house. As if he knew Frank was there watching him. Helen nudged him. He hadn't noticed her when she came and stood beside him. "Now you've gone and done it," she said. "I can see it in his face."

He couldn't sleep that night. He lay there instead and listened to her breathe. She was ninety pounds at most, but there was nothing frail about her. He turned his pillow around so it was cool against his skin. All her talk about Travis had gotten his heart racing. He could feel it sometimes. It fluttered like a bird against his ribs, and one day it would betray him. She'd be a widow then. She'd have to take care of the house herself.

He rolled to his side and pushed himself up. The bed springs creaked, but she didn't stir, not even when he knocked against the nightstand on his way to the window. Her breathing was deep and steady, just a little quieter than a snore. He sat down in the reading chair where she liked to do her crosswords. It was the best spot in the house, that's what she always said. She could see the pots of lavender from there and her sweet peas and climbing roses.

He stretched his legs out. A miller was flying in the room. It hovered in the amber glow of the nightlight. He tried to catch it. They made a mess, those moths. They fouled up his white walls. It flew upward and into the curtains, and he was reaching for it when he saw something outside. A hint of movement. A shadow beside his pond where there weren't any trees. He leaned in closer and saw the orange glow of a cigarette. It moved in the dark like a firefly, and then it went out.

Helen shouted when she saw the fish. She yelled for him to hurry. The pond was soapy. He saw the bubbles and the foam and then their pale bellies floating upward in the water. He pulled them out one by one. They were ten years old, some of them, and they might have lived another twenty. They might have outlived him and Helen both. Helen was weeping. He hadn't seen her cry in years, and now the tears were rolling down both her cheeks. *What a waste*, she was saying. *What a shame.*

He gathered them up and burned them in the fire pit. He sat in his chair and watched the smoke wind upward and it should have been a cloudy day. There should have been a storm coming with thunderclaps and lightning, but the sky was as blue as ever and the first tulips were starting to bloom. When the fire had burned itself out, he went around the garden and gathered all the butts Travis had dropped on their lawn.

The officer wore a gold wedding band, but he looked as young as the high school kids who loitered in the malls. Maybe it was the freckles or his spiky hair. He sat at their kitchen table, and Helen refilled his coffee cup before it was half empty. He took down all the information, writing it in neat block letters.

"Could you tell who it was," the young officer asked. His name tag said Dunn, but he asked them to call him Marcus. "Could you see his face?"

"I didn't need to see his face," Frank said. "My neighbor he smokes those sweet spice cigarettes." He took out the Ziploc bag with the butts from his garden and set it on the table. "He was home last night. He works four days on and three off."

"I haven't seen ones like that before." Officer Dunn reached for the baggie. He took a reluctant sniff.

"He drops those black butts all over his yard, and now he's coming here. Three o'clock in the morning and I see his cigarette burning in my yard."

Dunn wrote it all down and looked at the ashes where the fish were burned and the soap foam on the water. The lilies had turned yellow already. Their leaves drooped in the water, and the spotted frogs were gone, Frank noticed this just now. The garden was too quiet without them. Dunn crouched to see where the butts had been dropped. He walked the perimeter of the garden and opened up the gardening shed and the back gate. He poked around the bushes, too, and in the flower pots.

Then he went next door and rang the Fishers' bell. When nobody answered, he opened up the screen and knocked on the wooden door. Nobody came, and no curtains moved. They were home, Frank knew this. They were right inside their house, and they didn't open the door for an officer of the law. Dunn walked back to his cruiser. He waited there for a while and took down some more notes. The radio on his belt was crackling. Frank came and stood with him.

"They're home," Frank said. "I know it for a fact." Travis's truck was there in the driveway, and he probably wasn't even sleeping yet.

"I'll come back," Dunn said. "I'll come tomorrow and see if I can find him." He reached for the handle to the cruiser door. He looked at the fence Frank had built and how it ended at the boat. "I'm sorry about your fish." He seemed sincere the way he said it.

"Every year I drained that pond. I kept it clean for them."

Dunn nodded. "People can be jealous. They see something nice and it rankles." He climbed inside and shut the door. He knocked against the glass before he pulled away. He opened his window halfway down. "It might take some time, but we'll settle this. Keep your distance in the meanwhile." He cocked his head. "I'd hate to see things spiral." He pulled away, waving his hand from the open window, but he didn't return Frank's calls, and he didn't come back, not the next day or the day after that.

Frank saw the cigarette again just before the Fourth of July. He saw it from their bedroom window. He went down the hall and through the kitchen without turning on the lights. He grabbed his wooden walking stick because he didn't have his revolver anymore. Helen wanted no handguns in the house. She didn't mind his air gun, but it was down in the basement, packed up in its case. He carried the walking stick in both his hands and went out the back door. The motion lights above the deck came on as he passed. They lit up the yard and the vegetable beds. He could see all the way back to the trees where the cigarette had been.

"Get back here." He ran toward the fence. "I see you. I see just where you are." He yelled loud as he could. The lights were coming on in the houses behind him and the ones next door. The young couple in the Shrever house stepped onto their porch. Helen was coming out now, too. Her hair in those big curlers, and she hadn't even stopped to put her slippers on.

"Come back," he shouted, and he swung his stick around. "You can't hide from me." He was short of breath. He gasped and couldn't find any air.

Helen led him back inside. She took the stick from him and set it down, and she heated up some milk for him and sweetened it with honey.

"It's no good what you're doing. You're going to get yourself hurt," she said. "We need to think this through." She brought him his cup and sat with him at the table. She talked about townhouses again, all those nice ones they were building off Powers and Academy. The master sergeant was up there. He grew his tomatoes on the balcony now. He had one of those hydroponic systems, and it was nicer than a garden. Not even two inches of snow, and the management boys were out there shoveling.

He pretended to listen to what she said. He waited for her to finish. "Go back to bed," he said. "I'll be along in a bit." He should have been grateful she was there with him. She was better than he deserved, but he felt only anger at her curlers and her tired eyes and how she'd pestered him years ago to sell his old revolver. He waited until she was asleep before he climbed beside her.

Every Tuesday morning Helen took her military ID and went to Walgreens for the discount. She'd be gone an hour or maybe two if she met someone there she knew. He brought the air gun out as soon as she'd left. He set the stock against his hip and broke the barrel open. He had a Beeman gun, and it was quiet when it shot. He took a handful of pellets from the tin. He dropped all but one into his shirt pocket. He set a single pellet in and pulled the barrel back until it locked.

There was nobody in the yard next door. Travis was probably sleeping, and his wife was somewhere inside. He carried the rifle through his back door, past the deck and the empty pond. He didn't look down at the water. He went to the gardening shed near the back fence. He'd built it for Helen almost twenty years before, and it was time to paint the door again and the window boxes. He walked back and forth behind the shed until he found the best spot.

He shouldered the rifle and pointed it toward the Fishers' maple tree. The crows were up high in the branches. He looked through the scope. He wasn't more than thirty yards away, and he could see all their feathers and how they shone blue. The gun made only a soft sound when he fired. Only a whoosh and a bird fell from the branch. It fell with one wing open and whirled downward to the grass. The other crows were riled. They cawed and flapped their wings and flew upward all at once. More birds came from other trees and circled the maple. He reached for another pellet. He crouched behind Helen's shed and waited for them to settle down. He'd get a half dozen more if he was patient. Let the cats eat the birds he killed. Let them stay out of his yard for once and choke on the bones. He thought these things and regretted them, and for the first time since the war his hands trembled when he held his gun.

The bail bondsman put his house up for sale from one day to the next. His back was still in a brace from the disc surgery, but he pounded in the sign himself. He waved at Frank when he was done and shrugged a little. It was the only other house left on the block that still had a lawn and flower beds. "It's time," he shouted from across the street. "We're moving out to Calhan. We've got some acres there."

Frank waved back and went inside with his paper. He sat in the living room which they never used because the TV was in the kitchen. He looked around at the things they'd collected. Helen's showcase with her figurines and her watercolors. She liked to paint roses and hydrangeas in round vases, and she'd taken classes over the years at the community college. The first few were horrible and not even he could muster up a compliment and make it sound sincere, but she'd gotten better now and the flowers looked almost real. He stretched his legs out on the ottoman. He'd put up paneling in '73 and laid down wall-to-wall shag, and he took it all out again ten years later and refinished the oak floors. He hung lamps where she wanted them and painted the walls, and he'd made an entryway by framing out a wall and hanging it with paisley paper. It was their paradise, this house.

He opened the newspaper across his lap. Just last night somebody took a gun into the Radisson and shot the desk clerk dead. Gangs were coming in from Chicago and from Los Angeles, the police chief was saying. They were shooting each other even in the daytime. It made him tired to read the stories. The city was changing, and he wanted to lie down. He wanted things to stay the way they were. Every month another house sold, and the new people who came didn't water their gardens or sit in front on their lawn chairs. They parked snow mobiles and broken trucks in the middle of their yards, and their children had no manners. Always running and shouting even at ten o'clock at night. They ran outside when it rained and splashed barefoot in the storm gutters, and they were going to cut themselves one day. They were going to get infected.

The clock chimed in the hallway, and it sounded like a church bell. He folded up the paper and set it aside. It was better not to know. He wasn't fast the way he used to be, and things kept moving anyway. They were pulling him along. His boy would be almost forty. He'd have gray hairs of his own.

Helen came in from the garden with cut roses and tiger lilies. She whistled while she filled the vase. She jumped when she saw him sitting in the chair. "I didn't know you were in here," she told him. "You gave me a little scare." She tilted her head, and when he didn't say anything she came to him and put her hands on both his shoulders. He wondered if she ever thought about their boy. He wanted to know, but he would never ask.

•

They were up on the corner when they first heard the sirens. Fire trucks lined both sides of their street. He parked three houses up, and he hadn't unlatched his seat belt yet and Helen was off running. She was quick even in her stockings and her church shoes. By the time he caught up, her eyes were red from the smoke. She was stopped in the middle of the street. They stood together in front of their house and watched it burn. Sparks fluttered in the air and fell back down. The firemen uncoiled the hoses. They ran for the hydrant, and one of them shouted and waved his hands.

Helen pulled him. "We've got to move," she said. "They're telling us to go." He let her take him by the arm, and they went to the bail bondsman's porch and stood there on the steps. The engine driver was on top working the panel, and the others ran with the nozzles. It didn't even take a minute and the water arced high over their roof. The streams met and crossed, and it was almost like a fountain how they danced in the air. She was telling him something. He could hear her voice and how calm it was. She pointed and shook her head, but he didn't listen. All he could see was the firemen and how they ran across his grass in their boots and trampled his blooming lilies.

It began on the deck. He learned this only later. Travis must have waited for them to leave for church, and then he'd jumped the fence one last time. The cushions on the loungers must have gone up first and then the firewood they'd stacked against the deck. The junipers in the rock beds would be next and the ponderosa pine that grew beside the house. It was dry that tree and always dropped its needles. He should have cut it down. Helen had said so more than once, but he'd left it because it was beautiful.

The wind blew the sparks upward. It carried them to the roof tiles and into the attic vents, and that's where they must have found a place. They shuddered and grew, and the house burned from the inside out. The windows broke one after the next. The beams burned and the interior walls and only the brick was left untouched, those pale gray and pink bricks that nobody else had, not on any of the streets.

The firemen moved faster now. They were running around like soldiers. The hydrant wasn't enough anymore, and they used the tanker and all the pumps. Everybody from the nearest houses came out to the street and watched. Everybody except the Fishers, whose truck was gone. The neighbors' kids ran along the walk. They shouted and pointed. It was better than fireworks or a carnival seeing those trucks up close and how the flames moved in the wind.

"They're wrecking all my lilies," he said. "Look how they're crushing them down."

She shook her head at that. She looked a little worried. "Sit," she said. "You need to sit for a while." But he didn't move and he didn't budge and he watched the flames instead. The wind gusted beneath his jacket. One of those dry mountain winds that come in May and last until August and dry out all his beds. Always blowing. Always bending the treetops and clearing the clouds from the sky.

The fence was burning, that picket fence he'd just built. It burned before he'd even painted it, and the old tarp that covered the boat went next and then the boat itself. The fuel tank and the lines went up because Travis hadn't drained them. Burning pieces of fiberglass went high into the trees, and the steering wheel flew like a Frisbee over the street. *Sweet mother Mary*, Helen was saying, *sweet Mary look at that.* Her hands were over her mouth.

The firemen added more hoses, but all their water didn't stop the flames or the smoke cloud that mushroomed over the treetops. Blacker than asphalt that smoke and he could taste it in his throat. Every time he thought they had the fire doused, it began to burn again. He'd never seen anything burn like that boat, not even in the army. It must have been the resin in the fiberglass. It turned into a powder.

He climbed down the steps and across the bondsman's lawn and stood beside the For Sale sign. More sparks were coming. The trees were shedding them like leaves. Firebrands fell over the Fishers' yard and onto their sloping roof. He knew what would happen next. Travis was lazy with his gutters. Ponderosa needles were up there and dried bird nests and the accumulated leaves of a dozen years. They burned now with a popping sound like a thousand cap guns, and the flames swayed in the wind and moved across to the wooden eaves. For the first time the firemen were really shouting. The leader ran for the truck. They turned their cannon toward the Fisher house because it was wood that house and so was the next one up. They swiveled it until the aim was right, and the water came out like fifty hoses combined.

The foam came next. The firemen filled both houses like cream puffs. Some of the neighbors came and shook his hand or patted him on the shoulder. "We'll be alright," he told them. "We'll build her back better than she was." He talked about adding a gazebo this time and a covered porch out back, and they'd put metal screens on all the attic vents. It wasn't true, he knew this already. In September he'd be eighty-four, and Helen had started circling ads in the real estate section and leaving them by his chair. For planned communities with recreation centers and art tours of the city and bus trips to New England to see the falling leaves. "By Christmas we'll be back," he said. "Maybe even sooner." The neighbors looked doubtful, but they nodded anyway.

The firemen had begun to coil their hoses. A few were in his yard again and stepping on his lilies. They were breaking all the rose plants, and his lawn had turned to mud. Only the maple tree behind the Fisher house was untouched. Not even its crown was scorched. Another day or maybe two and the crows would come back in its branches. He looked at the tree and the twisted husk of the boat. It was too bad Travis hadn't stayed to watch.

She came up beside him. "I've talked to the Musselmans," she said. "They've got the air bed ready." She stepped back and gave him a hard look. "Why are you smiling? You're scaring me." She touched his forehead with her fingertips, and they were cool against his skin. It was time to leave. It was time to go, but she looked so young just then. She looked how she did when they'd first met in school, and he reached for her hand and held it.

Tremble

His hands began to shake again in the Safeway checkout line. The woman in front had eighteen items when the limit was fifteen. Diapers and canned soups and a shabby head of lettuce. Comet and ten different Weight Watchers dinners, and her baby was crying in its seat. It wailed just like a siren. His hands shook so hard he almost dropped his wallet. The regular cashier was gone, the pretty Korean lady with the long black hair. This new one had a goiter. He looked around at the other aisles, but they were just as busy. He had to stay because he needed turkey to make his chili. That's the only reason he came. Turkey and kidney beans and a fat green pepper, but not any spices. He ordered those on the Internet because he didn't like those cheap glass bottles. The light stripped out all their flavors. Might as well use wood shavings the way they tasted.

The mother up front was looking for her Club Card. "It's in here somewhere," she said. "I can never find things in this purse." She wore a blue down parka that was torn at the collar. Her boots were wet from the melting snow. Her baby was still crying, and people two aisles over were starting to look, but she didn't seem to care.

She started to empty out her bag, a dirty suede bag that needed the brush. She fished out a Kleenex wad and a pair of rusty nail clippers, a cigarette lighter, and a comb. She put these things on the little platform where people signed their checks. "I saw it just the other day," she was saying. An asthma inhaler came next, some baby wipes, a Ziploc bag with coupons. She lifted up her bag sideways so she could see inside it better, and it was too much, the mess she was making. He felt a throbbing behind his eyes.

He reached inside his wallet. He took a five dollar bill and set it on the belt. "Here you go," he said. He looked at the lady but not the crying baby with its perfect little fists. Her hair was oily and stuck to her forehead. It was blond in places, but the ends were brown. No telling what color it had been when she was little. "Forget about the card."

The mother looked at the crisp bill. "I don't need your money."

"It's more than you'd get if you used your card."

"How would you know a thing like that?"

"You're holding up the line," he said. There was nobody behind him.

She pushed her cart forward. "I don't want your money."

The cashier reached for a metal ring with cards hanging from it. "Ma'am," she said. "I've got a blank one right here." She swiped the card over the scanner.

There wasn't any checker so the cashier bagged the groceries herself. She mixed the lettuce with the Comet, but the mother didn't complain. The cashier set the bags in the cart and looked at the receipt before handing it over. Her goiter was big as an apricot.

He set his items on the belt while the mother gathered up her things. He dropped his basket on top of the others and straightened up the stack so people wouldn't trip. He had only three things and look how long he'd waited. He pointed to the Express Lane sign. "Next time pay attention," he said to the mother, who was zipping up her parka. He stepped a little closer. "Can't you read the sign?"

"Don't go pointing at me," she said. "You need to learn some manners." Her baby was wheezing. It hit the handlebar of the cart like a tiny drummer, and she squared her shoulders and pushed her cart past the aisle and through the double doors.

She was in the parking lot when he came out with his bag. She was only a few cars down. She drove a rusty Datsun that might have been green once. She strapped her baby in its seat and left her empty cart pushed up against another car. She was a sign of how things were going, another symptom of a general disease. He set his bag in the passenger seat. He scraped the ice from his windshield, and his hands shook even harder from the cold. People didn't pay attention to the rules. They made right turns from the left-hand lane, even when it snowed. They pulled out into the street without looking because what did it matter if somebody had to hit their brakes. What did it matter if they used the parking lane to cut their way to the front. Pornography on the billboards. Ladies with their mouths open and their hair looked bleached and ironed flat like the bristles of a broom, and he didn't want to see them.

She took Circle all the way to Highway 115 and then east toward Fort Carson. He could see the sticker on her window now that he was close. She was married to a soldier and she should shop in the commissary and not at Safeway. She should stay where she belonged. They passed the new apartments that were coming up on both sides of the highway. Mushroom-colored buildings with names like Gold Rush and Wildridge Meadows. She turned left at the gate and the MPs waved her through, and he kept on going. It was another half mile before he could turn around.

The checker at King Soopers with the scar above her lip. The Mexican girls walking home from Mitchell. They wore short skirts even in December. The lady selling roses outside the Guadalupe Church. Nothing was better than their Aztec hair. Those slanting indio eyes. All the mothers pushing their strollers around Memorial Lake. They were fifteen, sixteen, they weren't even twenty. He wanted to warn them the trail wasn't safe. They needed to walk in groups.

He used his mother's copper pot. She'd never measured anything. She went only by taste. *You have to cook with love and not with those recipe books*, she'd say. She taught him how to make the stock when he was eleven. They stood together in front of the stove, and her skin was shiny from the steam. Her hair was long back then. She wore it in a bun, but the ringlets came loose from the band and curled against her neck. He was on the step stool and she was there behind him, and he could feel her breath against his cheek while she told him what to do.

He chopped the bell pepper and the onion and he minced the garlic on his board. He worked in his white undershirt because it was warm inside the kitchen. He didn't skimp on heating. He'd kept it warm for his mother when she was sick, and he kept it warm now that she was gone. He rinsed the beans, and he seeded the jalapeño and chopped it superfine. His shaking stopped when he worked the knife. His hands were always steady once he knew what he was doing.

Sweet Deepa with her shiny hair. Look at her by the sink. Washing those containers from her lunch and the whole office smelled like incense from the spices. That's the way her house probably smelled, too. Her house and her skin, and he wanted to follow her home. She lived in an apartment off Murray. She kept a bicycle on her balcony, but he'd never seen her ride it. He stood by the vending machines and pretended to look at the chips, but he was watching her instead and how she'd pushed her sleeves back to her elbows. Skin dark as chocolate and the water ran down her forearms. Deepa and Loretta with her strawberry hair and all the girls who walked between the bays. They smelled like shampoo when he came close. They smelled so clean until they got engaged.

He dug his hands deep in his pockets to stop them from shaking. He pretended to dig around for change. Even in the lunchroom he could hear the humming from the phones, all those voices saying the same things, and some were laughing and some tried to sound sexy, but Deepa's voice was different when she worked her lines. It flowed like water. It rose and fell, and she was so serious when she talked. Sometimes he took the long way to the men's room just to get close enough to hear. She'd come 8,445 miles from Bombay to Colorado. He'd looked it up on the net. She'd come halfway around the world, and now it was winter and she could be answering phones in India where it was always warm.

She finished drying her stainless steel containers and packed them in her canvas bag. Her hair was loose today and not back in a braid the way he liked it. He came beside her and opened the fridge. He was close enough to touch her. He could brush against her shoulder if he wanted. She was wearing her pale blue sweater, and it had started to pile down the sides where her arms had rubbed. He could

touch the wool of it and that long black hair. She didn't gossip with
the other girls or go outside for a smoke. She didn't have a boyfriend.
He knew these things. He tried to stand straight because that way he'd
look thinner, but he was enormous, big as a house. If somebody cut
him, he'd bleed gravy.

He reached for his strawberry yogurt. He kept it in the back, and
when he pulled it out it was lighter than it should be. Somebody had
peeled away the foil. They'd eaten half his yogurt before putting it back
inside the fridge. His hands shook at the wrongness of it. It was only a
little thing, but his hands shook and he had to steady himself against
the wall. He went to the Whole Foods on Academy just to get those
Australian yogurts. They had pectin and not gelatin like the cheap ones
they sold at Safeway. His legs shook, too, and he couldn't still them.
When he came back into the main room the voices hit him like a wave.

His mother's hair had been beautiful before the surgeons took it.
Sometimes he'd watched her brush it. He held her braid when he first
learned to swim. He was seven, almost eight, and they went to the
outdoor pool at the Satellite every afternoon. She knew the doorman
there, an old man from Madrid who didn't care if they weren't guests.
She smiled and the doorman smiled, too, and opened the gate for her.
Come on, Lenny, she'd say. *Before it gets too busy.* She carried him on
her back and went below the water, and the world went silent in that
moment. Her skin was waxy against his. He grabbed her braid, that
fat black braid. *It's easy,* she said. *This is how we were a million years
ago. Just a momma monkey and her baby in the water.* She laughed the
way she sometimes did. Her hair was almost blue. She looked like a
mermaid or those carvings on the front of ships. The olive skin she
got from her grandma who came from Jalisco. She lay beside him on
the lounge and talked about Nagual who could turn into a puma and
Cihuacoatl who went to the crossroads at night. Poor Cihuacoatl who
waited for her baby boy, but all she found there was a knife.

They ate his chili next. He went to his table to pick up his thermos,
and someone had eaten the chili from inside and left the dirty spoon.

They'd taken his apple, too, and squeezed the jelly beans from the goose his mother had crocheted. He kept it beside his monitor. They emptied it out and didn't refill it, and they did it because he was fat. They did it because the regular chairs weren't big enough and he used a special rolling chair from Widebodies that didn't pinch his thighs. He needed to get a hidden camera or maybe some ipecac to put in his thermos, and they'd be sorry then. He wanted to burn them with hot peppers.

He sat down in his chair, and Loretta was laughing in the corner. She was waving her fat hands, and Deepa was working a call and her face was serious the way it gets, and someone had burnt their Lean Cuisine. There was shouting in the lunchroom. Dilman the next table over had taken off his boots again and now the room smelled like feet. He knew this place. All its sounds and its voices, the way the sun came through the windows at three every afternoon. He knew it when it was full with people and when he was there alone, and some day this place would burn or a shooter would find his way inside.

There was a poster beside the coffeemaker in the employee kitchen. It said to take the stairwell in case of fire and to turn off your cell phone if somebody is shooting. Turn it to vibrate so the shooter won't hear and then wait until he reloads. That was the time to run. Active shooters and suspicious behavior and all the tips wouldn't help. They were sitting at round tables. They were wearing headsets, and there wasn't any place to run. The doors were at the end of the room, and the stairwells were too narrow. One day it would happen. Someone would come through the double doors. Someone with a loaded gun, and he needed to keep Deepa safe.

Deepa kept her hairbrush in a sandalwood box beside her keyboard. It was half past three in the morning, and the office was empty. That's when he liked to look. He swiped his card and opened the doors, and he walked between all the tables before coming to her spot. He opened that box, and she had chewing gum in there from Cadbury's India and extra hairbands and a photograph of a little girl standing next to a carved stone wall. Elephants and dancing ladies with long long hair and the girl stood right between them. Little Deepa when she wore knee socks. She looked straight at the camera, and he knew her from her eyes.

He pulled a few strands from the hairbrush. She would never know. That heavy hair that spilled down her back. It shone even under the fluorescent lights. Imagine her in the water. Just think how it would shine. He pulled the strands out from the bristles and cupped them in his palm. The old security guard was gone. He never made his rounds. He was probably sleeping down at his desk. Sometimes he left for Denny's and ate nachos instead of watching the doors.

Deepa's chair was too small for him, but he sat down anyway and looked around the room. It smelled like coffee and microwave popcorn. The monitors glowed blue. This was where Deepa sat, and it wasn't right how she couldn't see the window. He needed to bring her a present and leave it on her chair, a box of caramels or a bromeliad from Safeway, a purple phalaenopsis like the ones she knew from home. He needed to hurry. He wasn't getting any younger. All the girls and he remembered where they sat and how their voices sounded. Before Deepa there had been Marta, whose family was Italian. Marta and Pilar and Tina with her strange gold eyes. They came, those girls, they came with their long dark hair and then they went away.

The widow who cried when he asked for her dead husband and the man who shouted about acid rain and mercury in the water. One old lady thought he was her son. *Freddy, you never call me anymore*, she said. *Don't you love your momma?* The babies wailing and the sirens through the line and all the people who cursed him for interrupting their supper. A man who laughed and laughed at the sound of Leonard's voice. Maybe he was Armenian. *Te zent tartakuti*, he said, and it sounded like a curse.

Deepa was wearing a new locket on a thin gold chain. She touched it with her thumb. He was coming back from the men's room when he saw it. His hands were still wet from the sink. It was a present, he was certain. Somebody had bought her that engraved locket, and she'd lifted her hair so he could put it around her neck. She touched it with her thumb and her eyes were closed while she worked her call. He wanted to stop beside her table so he could pull it off her neck, but he kept on walking and sat down in his chair.

The woman who answered couldn't see his shaking hands or how the carpet tiles were stained. How the new girl across the table chewed her nails and spit the pieces in the trash. Her hair was so short she might as well shave the rest of it off. She was probably a lesbian. "Who is this," the woman said. There was yelling in the background and the sound of the TV.

"It's Leonard Spivvy at Peak Marketing. We're an investment information. . . ."

"Jacob, put that marker down."

"We're an investment information service," he said.

"Do you hear me? That one's a Sharpie and it won't come off."

"We provide courtesy investment information for you in the form of a prospectus."

"Who is this?" she asked again. Her voice was even sharper now. Someone was banging the walls at her house. Someone was really shouting.

"Basically we work with a group. And we offer folks like you the chance to participate in a real estate project or a trust possibly with a new company just starting—"

"Jacob Oren Goodman, if you don't come here this second I swear I will take away the controls. No games for a month."

His hands were starting to shake harder. He wasn't sure why. That boy was screaming when he should listen to his mother. "You need to whip him," he said.

"What? What did you say?"

"You need to use the strap—"

She hung up so hard he felt the concussion through his head-set. He rubbed his temples because that's where he kept his tension. The girl behind him was using her flirty voice. She was laughing like somebody on a date. Thirty people talking on the phone and they were all following the script. Somebody across the room had found an investor, and a few people were applauding. This is how his days would go. The weeks and months and years. He'd sit there from noon until eight in the evening. He'd push the numbers as they came up, and he'd make his calls until somebody stopped him.

It was the seventh of March the last time he held his mother's hand. It was half past eight in the morning. The flakes were falling outside. All night it had been snowing, and the roads filled faster than the plows could clear them. There weren't any doctors in the halls. The hospital was quiet. He held her hand and she lay there breathing. There was a bandage on her scalp from where they'd made the incision. She was sixty-three, but she looked ageless beneath the blanket. Like a girl. Like an ancient woman and her skin had lost its wrinkles and its color. It had gone completely smooth. The world was white outside the window. The sky was white and the dead grass in the courtyard and the mountains were hidden behind clouds, and he sat on a stool beside her bed. He held her right hand because the left one had the tubes. It was eight thirty in the morning and the snow was falling and he held that hand. It trembled and went still.

Deepa deserved better than those motorcycles in the lot and the rusty green dumpsters. Sagging sofas on the curb stained black from the melting snow. Soldiers lived there, young GIs who looked fifteen in their uniforms, and it wasn't safe a girl alone like that with all those men around. They drank beer on the weekends and did pull-ups on the clothesline posts just because they could. They walked around in summertime with all their muscles showing. He sat in his car and watched her window. He knew the best places to park. Sometimes she stood on the balcony and looked out toward the mountains.

He turned his collar up. Snow was coming in again, he could feel it in the air. He'd have to scrape his window before he left. People still had their Christmas lights up. It would be March before they took them down. Some people would leave them up all year, and there was nothing sadder than Christmas lights in May. The world was full of lazy people. His mother said loneliness was a disease. She said it was catching like the flu, but loneliness was a blessing. There were people everywhere he looked.

A man stepped out on the balcony where Deepa kept her bike. He wore boxer shorts and a white T-shirt, and even from across the street Leonard could see how his arms were ropy with muscle. He didn't seem to feel the cold. Deepa came out in a robe. She was holding a coffee mug, and she pulled him back inside. The man laughed. He pretended to pull back before letting her win. They went inside and he could see them through the glass, how they pushed and pulled each other in circles. Deepa smiled and threw back her head. She laughed for this man who didn't deserve her. She told him all her secrets. They were dancing in her kitchen, and one day that building would burn. It was made of wood and the roof was, too, and it wouldn't take much, just a rag and some kerosene, and somebody would do it and he wouldn't save her, that man with the muscles. He wouldn't lift a finger.

Hotel fires. Steam pipe explosions. Twenty-three dead on Weber because somebody was frying a turkey. A special ed bus overturned when the driver had a seizure. Stampedes at Walmart. A little boy at Fort Carson who found his daddy's gun. A coffee cup wedged under a brake pedal. Acre upon acre of forest gone. A lady park ranger had been burning her husband's letters. Girls abducted from the swimming pool. Patients at the nursing home smothered in their sleep. Christmas trees going up like torches. Especially those Scotch pines. The billboards, everywhere the billboards, and there wasn't any quiet and there wasn't any peace, not even when he tapped the walls or rocked in his mother's chair. Everything ends, that was the lesson. The city was burning and nobody noticed. There wasn't any place left to go.

She was wearing silver shorts today, and her nails were painted white. The others called her Bibi, but he never said her name. He shouldn't have come. Three months resisting the pull and he needed to be stronger. He should be home filing his bills. He had entire folders waiting to be shredded, but he parked his car in the gravel lot and walked inside to find her. She led him down the hall. There were girls dancing in the mirrored rooms. He tried not to look as he went by. Those girls with their ironed blond hair that looked stiff even in the flashing lights. Their skin was too pale or too orange from the bronzer. Their nipples were too pink. They moved their hips and they took their bras off and the men sat in their chairs as if crippled by the sight of them. Like paralytics at the gates of heaven. The women danced and touched themselves. They leaned close to the men and pulled away. They crouched like cats across that sticky floor and their backs were always arched, and he wanted to cover them.

She had chicken pox scars on her temples. He knew each one. He knew the tattoos on her hip and he wished them away. Her hair was wavy, and it came to the small of her back. She took him to the room and sat on a metal stool. There were mirrors on three of the walls and a sagging velvet couch. He combed the spray from her black hair. He started at the bottom and worked his way upward through the tangles. He divided her hair into three parts when it was ready, feeling them by weight to make sure they were even. He braided the plaits. He started low at the nape of her neck so it wouldn't hurt her or pull at her skin. The music went quiet as he worked. The room was full with the sound of his beating heart, and for a little while he wasn't fat; no, he was slender the way he used to be, and his hands stopped all their shaking.

She sat still for him when he was done. He watched her in the mirror. The ovals of her breasts and those chocolate-colored nipples. Big as half dollars and her chest rose and fell with every breath. He stood above her and looked at her fat braid and it was perfect how it dangled. He needed things to stop for a while. He needed to close his eyes. It was three o'clock and the sun was shining off the water and the concrete was rough beside the pool so people wouldn't slip. The smell of coconut lotion and chlorine from the water, and she was getting up. She was always getting up. Their time was done, and she was looking at herself in the mirror. He would have given her a hundred dollars, but she asked only for twenty.

Dead Languages

She hadn't put down the grocery bags when her boy finally began to talk. She hadn't even closed the door. He stood there sure as the pope and pointed at her with sticky fingers. *Apo*, her little Nicholas said. He looked at the ceiling, and his eyes were shut. *Apo tou nun epi ton hapanta.* It sounded like a song. It sounded like the martial arts movies Gary liked to watch. She dropped her bags at the sound. She let them fall to the kitchen tiles, and the eggs broke and seeped through the paper.

More than two years she'd waited for him to speak. She'd checked all her parenting books and wrote in her journal, and she waited for a syllable, for any sound at all. The Binghams' little girl was putting whole sentences together. She was singing along with the TV, and people said not to worry. *Boys can be slow that way, Holly. He's not a talker but look how he walks. Look at his sturdy legs.* They only made her more nervous how they tried to comfort her. She worked harder to coax the syllables out. She talked to him while she pushed his stroller along the streets. She pointed to the maples and the mountains and bulldozers on the street. She asked him questions, and he looked at her with those shiny eyes and his mouth made a perfect pink O. She answered her own questions and talked some more, and she sang even though her voice was awful. At night while he slept she whispered things into his ear. With Gary's long hours and only her voice in the house, she was getting a little strange. She wondered more than once if she was helping him. But now her boy was standing there, and the words were coming out in a jumble.

"Look at you," she said. She went to him and knelt. She didn't touch him or reach for him. Better not to scare him.

Sebastou, he was saying now. *Sebastou Germanikou,* and a little bubble of spit formed in the corner of his mouth. It didn't sound like Spanish, though the gardeners shouted every afternoon just outside his window. It didn't sound like any language she knew, but it didn't matter because he was making sounds. Thirty months of silence in the house and now her boy was trying to tell her something. Soon he'd be talking like Emily Bingham and all the other children who toddled in the park. He'd be pestering her for toys. He opened his eyes, those dark eyes that were nothing like hers and they weren't like Gary's either. He clenched his little fists and smiled.

His arms went tight sometimes when the words came. His eyes rolled back in his head. All those words, all those musical sounds. Their boy said them with conviction, and none of them made sense. Gary who never frowned and never worried had started to pace the floors. He hadn't looked this anxious since taking the bar exam. "It's like *The Exorcist,*" he said one evening. They were standing in the kitchen, and Nicholas was babbling in his chair. "We'll need a busload of priests to straighten him back out." Gary tugged at his spiky black hair. He made jokes when he was nervous. It was no different from a twitch, but still it wasn't right. She lifted Nicholas from his chair and carried him to his crib because she didn't want him to hear what his daddy was saying. She was mad when she loaded the dishwasher and when she wiped the table clean. It wasn't until Gary touched her hand that she began to cry.

They went together to the doctor. Even Gary had to admit it was time. Their pediatrician sent them to a psychiatrist and that doctor sent them to somebody else, and everyplace they went the doctors used the same words. ADHD and expressive vocabulary delays and phonological disorders. They talked about autism, all of them. They talked about its wide spectrum, and these words meant nothing when she saw her sweet boy's face and how his fingers curled around hers. He wasn't even three yet, and the specialists took blood samples and family histories and scanned his brain, and it looked like a watercolor against that black screen. It looked like a butterfly caught in a bowl.

The speech pathologist sent him to a young therapist who frightened him with her bulging blue eyes. There were toy trucks and bouncing balls and stuffed bunnies along the shelves, and he began to cry as soon as the therapist touched him. He wailed like a child being whipped. His arms went stiff again. He arched his back and shouted in his special language, and he didn't stop not even when Holly came running. He panted against her cheek.

A professor named Anastas had heard about her boy. His cousin was an X-ray technician who'd listened to Nicholas sing. The professor came to visit just before Christmas and sat in their family room. Holly held Nicholas on her lap. He rocked back and forth and talked in a low low voice. He was in his dream world again. He didn't even notice this stranger who leaned in close to hear.

"It's Greek," Anastas said. The light reflected against his glasses so Holly couldn't see his eyes. "It's Greek the way it must have sounded. He pronounces it with tones."

Anastas was too excited to drink the coffee Holly had poured. He stood up and sat back down. He tugged at the threads along his cuffs where his sweater was coming unraveled. It lost its tones over the years, he explained to Holly. Two thousand years ago it must have sounded something like Chinese. That's how Nicholas was talking. Like someone come from a time machine. He was reciting inscriptions. He was reading from letters that soldiers wrote. Greek soldiers in Egypt who wrote back to their wives.

"He's not reading," Holly said. "My boy is only two, and he's just talking. He's making up sounds in his head."

"The soldiers' letters are down in Tennessee." Anastas reached for his laptop. He shook his head as if to clear it. "They keep the papyrus in special rooms. The archeologists didn't know at first. They thought the letters were worthless. They were looking for gold and glass and pottery and not some scribbled notes." Anastas shook his head again. "They burned the papyrus for that sweet smell. That's why there's only a few left. A few when there were thousands."

"We've never been down South," Holly said. "Nicholas was born right here in the Springs." He was born at Penrose Hospital, and all the nurses said they'd never seen a better baby. Almost nine pounds and his eyes were already clear. They shone like the moon on water.

Anastas was setting up his recorder. He was opening up his laptop and untangling the cords. "He's a miracle. And it's not just Greek I hear. There are other languages, too."

"You need to leave," Holly told him. She pulled Nicholas closer to her chest. "You won't be recording him today."

She wasn't polite when she held the door. She didn't take his card. And though she needed to make dinner and the dirty laundry was mounded in front of the machine, she held Nicholas for hours that afternoon. She turned on the lights on the Christmas tree and rocked him until he slept. She sang to him. *Sleep, little boy, sleep. Your father's tending sheep. Your momma's shaking the tree and all the dreams fall deep.* She sang, and his little face went slack. She thought of burning paper, of smoke wisping round, and all the traces those people had left. They'd lingered for two thousand years, and with the strike of a match they were gone. She nuzzled her boy in the crux of his neck. She breathed in his sweet smell.

Greek, Aequian, and Etruscan. Dacian. Elymian, Faliscan, and Ligurian. There were so many more. Messapic, Minoan, Oscan, Umbrian. And more still. The names belonged to other planets and other worlds. They belonged to craters on the moon. The professors came to listen, and Gary let them in. *It's for science*, Gary said. *It's for their research*, and she tried not to be angry. He was looking for his son, that's how she thought of it. His son who sat all day and rocked in his chair. Who didn't play with the trucks they bought him, who didn't listen to music or clap his hands or sing. This was his way of keeping something when everything else was lost.

•

Healers came, too, and believers in reincarnation. Serious men in suits who tracked snow into the house. Women who wore beads and let their hair go long and gray. Gary listened to them when they talked about children who spoke languages from other lives. Who'd lived a thousand years before and remembered what they saw. *It happened on the Pentecost*, he said. *That's just how it went.* The Galileans spoke a dozen different languages so the visitors could understand. They spoke languages they'd never heard because that's how God wanted it. He talked about taking Nicholas to church, to have him feel the Spirit. He wasn't working long hours anymore. Most days he didn't go into the office. His cell phone was never charged.

He started studying ancient Greek. He bought some used workbooks and struggled with the letters. *I've never seen a language like this before*, he said. *It's even worse than law school.* He wrote in his notebooks and learned the words for *father* and *mother* and *son*, and Holly made him coffee. She kept quiet because what was there to say. If those professors couldn't reach him with all their expertise, then what hope was there for Gary, who'd almost failed college French.

He crouched before Nicholas when he was ready. He held his sheet of paper and cleared his throat. "I'm not so sure about the grammar," he said. "Guess we'll just have to see."

"Ego eimi sos pateras." He spoke loud as a preacher. "Pa-te-ras." He thumped his chest to emphasize each syllable, and Nicholas opened his eyes.

"Pou ei?" He reached for his boy's wrist. Where are you? "Pou ei?" Gary asked again, but Nicholas wasn't listening. No, Nicholas was starting to rock again. His head tilted to the side.

Gary read the rest of his notes. He'd written all sorts of questions for his boy. Questions and explanations and things to calm him down. *Your name is Nicholas. And here is your mother. She loves you. When are you coming home?* He said these things in Greek and sometimes he stuttered and had to begin again, and Nicholas closed his eyes. He slept in his little chair.

"It's a start," Gary said. He pushed himself up from the floor. "He heard me that first time. Did you see? Did you see how he paid attention?"

"Yes," she said, "yes. I saw it all," and Gary looked contented. He whistled a little under his breath. He opened his Greek grammar books and started where he'd stopped, and it looked like random scribbles from where she was. It looked strange and familiar both. He'd learn *all* the languages right up the tree, she could tell from the set of his jaw. He'd go backward in time to the beginning. Climbing up to catch his boy, who would always fall away.

She gave Nicholas an orange to hold, and he reached for it and smiled. Gary was waiting in the car outside, but she didn't try to hurry. Nicholas loved going to the grocery store. It calmed him even on bad days. He loved the fruits and the fine water mist from the sprayers. He swung his legs back and forth in the cart, and twice she had to straighten him out again and make sure his belt was latched. She picked some ears of corn. The beets looked good, and she filled up two bags with them so she could make a salad. Gary needed more vegetables. He spent too much time inside. His skin had gone from walnut to ivory, and the capillaries showed below his eyes. She needed to cook more often and clean up the house. She needed to put away the toys.

She was pulling a plastic bag off the dispenser when Nicholas dropped the orange. It rolled underneath the cart, and before she could pick it up he reached for her wrist and squeezed. He tilted his head. He looked at her and tightened his hold, and the expression in his eyes was something like surprise. He looked around the store. At the dented carts and the Easter lilies that were arranged beside the door. All the people in their muddy shoes, all their tired eyes. A little girl with red hair ran between the aisles. He looked at her and the ribbons in her braids and the way her dress swung around her knees. He squeezed harder and dug his nails into Holly's skin.

An older woman pushed her cart alongside them. "Excuse me," she said. "I need to get by." She was holding a folder full of coupons.

Holly didn't move, and she didn't answer. She stayed where she was, but Nicholas let her hand go anyway. He rolled back in his metal seat, and what she had seen in his eyes, whatever it was, had gone away.

"Nicholas," she said. "Come back to me." She set his hand around her wrist and held it there. Who knew the things he saw. His eyes were dark when he was born. Dark and without end. He'd looked right past her in the birthing room. Like a tiny astronaut or an ocean explorer. When the nurses set him in her arms, his fingers had curled around her thumb but only for a moment. He pulled away and raised his fist toward the ceiling as if to show her something. *Look*, he seemed to say, *look at what you're missing*, and she was certain then that she'd known him always and that he'd always be a stranger.

"Nicholas," she said again, "listen to your mama." She unbuckled the straps in the shopping cart and pulled him to her shoulder. "There's nothing for you there," but even as she said it she wondered if it was true. She rocked with him against the shopping cart. She stroked his curly hair.

Rise

He visited the city every night. He walked along its streets. His father lived there and the girl did, too, and the air smelled of cinnamon and salt from the water. He saw no cars and no bicycles anywhere, no other pedestrians strolling between the buildings. The rooflines grew lower as he came to the water. The asphalt was jagged and split. Sometimes he stepped into puddles or slipped where the road was muddy. Sometimes he took off his shoes. There were ladies behind the windows. They reached for him between the bars and tried to catch his arm. All around him there were flowers. Jasmine and plumeria and gardenias with their perfume. Guava and stephanotis, he knew them when he saw them. He knew all the birds and trees.

It was always summer in the city. The air was always warm. He couldn't find Leo or Gemini or Venus shining like the moon. He saw none of the southern constellations either, the ones he knew from books. He saw anchors and crosses and trailing vines. A moth opening its wings. *Remember these things*, he told himself. *Take them with you when you leave.*

The woman was waiting on the sand. She sat on a woven straw mat and strung blossoms from a basket, working them one into the next. *Sit for a while*, she said. Her skin was pale as the flowers she held. *We've been waiting here for hours.* Heat rose from the sand as if the earth itself were something living. He worked the blossoms onto the string, and his fingers were sticky from the petals. They worked together until the sun rose and the crickets stopped their singing.

Ruby opened the blinds so the sun could shine across the bed. She stood there in her leggings and her purple flannel robe. "Pretty good," she said. "I didn't even have to sing."

She hadn't combed her hair yet, and her curls looked electrified. The oatmeal was ready, but he needed to hurry because it was already half past seven.

The kitchen smelled like coffee when he came out. She needed two cups to clear the clouds from her eyes, that's what she always said. She stirred the brown sugar into the oatmeal and the dried blueberries and brought the bowls to the round table. "Maybe we'll go riding this weekend," she said. "Before it gets too cold."

"The Chicago deal is heating up."

"The air would do you good. It's better than the gym."

"I'll know by Friday how the weekend looks."

"Three thousand dollars for a tandem and now we never use it." She tapped her finger against her front tooth, the one she'd had capped when she broke it on a cherry stone. She watched him scrape the edges of his bowl. She thought he was depressed. She'd say so any time there was an opening. That's why he slept through his alarm clocks. Maybe he should see somebody because it wasn't good to keep things bottled up. His father had been like that and look how things had gone for him. A heart attack at sixty-three and the bypasses couldn't fix things once the damage was done. Nobody could help him, not even that specialist from Denver. It had been over a year, and she had a referral for somebody good. A therapist with experience in bereavement. *Go see him, Ethan,* she always said. *You can go at lunch if you want. Or when you're done for the day.*

She had so many ideas. They could bicycle for Alzheimer's or walk for ovarian cancer. It would do him good to give something back, and he'd say, *yes, that'd be great* and *maybe next year,* and how could she understand? She'd never been careless or unlucky. Everything she touched blossomed. Everything except for him. The African violets on the kitchen windowsill were blooming again, and last spring she'd built a greenhouse from a kit. She called it her church, and that's what it looked like. It glowed in the evening when she worked. She had cherry tomatoes growing in there and orchids in hanging pots. Strange prehistoric-looking things with open-mouthed blossoms. Their roots curled in the air. It smelled like mushrooms inside and rotting wood and something else he couldn't name. *Come with me,* she'd say. *Why don't you keep me company,* and he'd go no farther than the door.

"Those folks in Chicago can wait," she said. "A couple of hours on a Saturday won't make any difference."

"Two years away from the firm and you've forgotten what it's like." Ruby worked for a judge now. A Carter appointee with silver hair, and things were always quiet in his chambers. She wrote bench memos three days a week, and he didn't mind if she worked from home.

"I'm just trying to give you some perspective." She came up behind him to get his empty bowl and kissed him on top of his head.

Here's what he didn't tell her: Thank God for the clients in Chicago who yelled at him all day. It was October already, and the deal wasn't anywhere near closing. They still hadn't signed the letter of intent because one of the partners always had a problem. The indemnification provisions were too broad or too narrow and the definitions were unclear. He fixed each issue as it came up, but there was always another. Bless them because they filled his days. Bless the clients and the IRS and the treadmill at the gym. He ran until his T-shirt was soaked and stuck against his skin. He answered calls and wrote his memos and did pull-ups on the bar. He was exhausted by eight and asleep by nine, and that's where he found his peace.

She waited by the river and the reservoir and down along the sand. She waited only for him. She sat on a woven blanket, and the air was so heavy and still. *Don't you want to see your father,* she wanted to know. *Don't you want to meet my baby girl?* Farther down the men were coiling ropes. Their boats rocked in the black water. They were ferrymen and fishermen, and their work was done for the day. *Night has fallen around us. Set your work aside.* She closed her eyes when she sang. Her voice never wavered. *Sleep without any worries. I'll always be your bride.* She sang songs he'd never heard before, but he knew how they went.

He had four alarm clocks on his nightstand. He lined them up like soldiers. Analog and digital and an old-fashioned one with a bell and another that vibrated the whole mattress. The manufacturer called it the Sonic Boom. It was designed for narcoleptics and the hearing-impaired, but even on its highest setting it wasn't strong enough. Only Ruby could wake him up. She pulled up the blinds and shook him by the shoulder, and if that didn't work she sang all the songs he hated. "Feelings" and "My Sharona" and "Sometimes When We Touch," and her voice cracked on the high notes. She sang into his ear, and she looked so relieved when he opened his eyes.

The little girl had been wearing a yellow dress. He hadn't seen her as she crossed. Traffic was stopped in the right-hand lane, and he was talking with Ruby on the phone. She had the vegetables ready, but he needed to pick up a roasted chicken from King Soopers. One of the good ones this time and not one that was all dried out. He needed to pay attention. The law hadn't taken effect yet, and it was perfectly legal to use his cell. He changed lanes because those idiots would make him miss the light. He changed lanes because he was tired and because he was hungry and impatient and because there was no God.

The girl wore a yellow dress, and there were flowers on the skirt. He saw these things. The flowers and her lace socks and the book bag she swung in the air. Her older sister was a few steps behind. She was close enough to see but powerless to change things. The girl flew over his hood. She cracked the glass as she went upward. Light as a bird flushed from the bush. Light as a skipping stone. He knew what had happened before she came back down. He stopped the car and dropped his cell phone and ran back to where she was. She lay against a storm grate. Her long brown hair had come undone.

The older girl began to howl. A sound unlike any he'd heard

before. She went to her knees and covered her baby sister. A bus driver came and tried to help, but she pushed him away. She set her palms over her sister's nose and her bare feet and all the places she was bleeding. She moved her hands in circles. As if she could plug those holes and mend the bones where they had broken. She leaned over her sister and pressed herself against that still body, and it took three paramedics to pry her away.

They took their tandem out on Saturday and rode up to the reservoir. It was warm for late October, but the mountains already had some snow. Up on the hills the cottonwoods were turning. Delicate things those yellow leaves. They fluttered like paper wings. He was in front and Ruby in back, and they rode together like a single person. He'd bought the bike ten years before as their first anniversary present. He told her when there were bumps and when to ring the bell, and there were other couples, too, in matching bike shorts and tunics. Seven thousand feet above sea level with a sky so bright it hurt his eyes. "Look at that," Ruby was saying. "Look at the baby deer," and it came near the road and tilted its head and its mother was there beside it. Past barns that had lost their rooftops and cabins set back from the road and he could see the water in the distance. So blue it was almost black. Ruby once said they lived in the perfect place. Winters need to be cold and the summers hot, and the seasons give life its rhythm.

They found a shady spot and ate their turkey sandwiches. She'd put in chips and horseradish, and his eyes watered from the sting. She climbed on a rock when she was done with her meal. She pulled her knees close to her chest. "Maybe this will be your medicine," she said. "Just coming up here the two of us and sitting in the sun." Her nose was sunburnt, and she worked her jaw the way she did to keep from crying. He wanted to climb up beside her on the rock, but there was only room for one.

Good evening good night turn off the light. Sleep with the roses and rabbits tonight. She strung the blossoms, and her hands were white. A ladybug crawled across her cheek. There were more on the blanket, mounds of them moving in circles between the flowers. *You'll wake up tomorrow if God wants you to. Open your eyes and the sky will be blue.* She reached for his wrist with those long fingers. It was time to show him the water. Her baby girl was waiting beside the rocks. Her skin was cool despite the heat, but he pulled his hand away. He didn't want her to stop her singing. *There's no hurry,* she said. *I've got nothing here but time.* She closed her dark eyes and sang to him like a mother. She rocked him in her arms.

He saw a lady at the gym with an ankh tattoo at the nape of her neck. She was always there no matter when he went. Her black hair was shaved close to her head, and she never smiled or talked. She worked in with him on the machines sometimes. A slender woman with narrow fingers, but she lifted more than most guys, and once he saw her do handstand push-ups against the mirror. The lady with the tattoo and the two gay guys who were serious about their sets, the grandma who wore orange lipstick when she worked with her personal trainer. He knew them all and nobody ever said hello, and that was how he liked it. He varied his routine to keep his muscles guessing. Push-ups on the BOSU ball. Three sets of twenty with claps in between and he felt the stabbing in his shoulder blades before he was halfway through. Crabwalking across the gym's basketball court, one-legged squats, nine minutes jumping rope. One thousand three hundred and fifty jumps, and his knees popped sometimes from the strain. Push-ups with his arms extended. Fingertip push-ups when he felt strong, or push-ups on one hand. Straitjacket sit-ups with his arms hugged tight across his chest. Sometimes he could see his heart beating through his wet T-shirt. Who knew what kept it going.

Her hair had been long just like her daughter's. Her eyes were almost black. She carried a backpack, and it had red ladybugs stitched across it and a button that said Marisa. She cradled that bag in her arms, and she didn't look around the room, not at him or the nurses or the police officers who were still taking down notes. His lawyer was coming. Sid Taborsky from the firm who knew all about backdated stock options and Medicare fraud, and Sid was useless because the girl was dead and nothing mattered now. The woman stood alone in the corner. Her older girl wasn't there, and neither was her husband if she had one. She didn't look up when the doctors came and when they told her the news. She didn't cry, and she didn't move. *My baby's not dead,* she said. *My baby's right here,* and she held that bag when she went to her knees. She held it against her chest, and he looked at the oval of her face and those long white fingers and he almost believed her.

The corporate folks needed him in Chicago for three days. He had to hold some hands in person and not just over the phone. One of the equity holders in a subsidiary was having doubts about the deal. He wanted more changes to the disclosure schedule or he'd pull out and everyone would be left hanging. "Be careful with those guys," they told him the day before he left. "Spellman's a screamer. I saw him break a keyboard once when things didn't go his way." The next day he'd give away bottles of Oban scotch if he'd really crossed the line. That was his way of saying sorry.

Ruby helped pack his bags. She had the shaving kit ready, and she folded all his shirts, and she took him to the airport, too, so he wouldn't have to park. "Don't look so worried," she said when she stopped in front of the terminal. "I'll call you every morning. I'll wake you up just like I do at home." She grabbed his arm before he walked inside. "Make a muscle," she said. She leaned out the window to give him a kiss, and she looked so sweet with her eyes closed.

A bench with the girl's name at the Franklin School and a willow tree planted in her honor. Ruby arranged these things. Sid Taborsky worked out the settlement and the no contest plea. Funeral and medical costs and the loss of future earnings. A year without a driver's license and fifty thousand dollars restitution, and none of it was enough. He wrote a letter to the mother and to the sister. It said how sorry he was and how he thought of them every day, and Ruby said he should meet them in person and ask for forgiveness. She said it would make it easier to forgive himself, and maybe she was right. He dialed the number a dozen times but hung up before it rang.

He'd dreamt those first months of falling. He jumped from a plane and his chute wouldn't open. He was climbing rocks, and they were slick from the rain. He fell from windows and bridges and balconies, and he opened his arms the way divers do. He arced backward in the air. These thoughts calmed him. He walked at night, going as far as Prospect Lake where people kept pit bulls behind their fences. He stopped carrying his pocket knife or his can of pepper spray and he waited for something to happen, but nothing ever did.

Ruby said we have choices, each of us. *You have a choice just like your father did. He chose to smoke those cigarettes and to skip those doctor's appointments. Don't you make the same mistake.* He needed to do something good with the time he had. He owed it to himself and to that little girl, and it was easy for her to say that, his sweet Ruby whose plants were always blooming. Who took yoga every Thursday at the courthouse gym. She'd gone to visit his father those last few months. She tried to get Ethan to come along, but he always found a reason not to. Tip her over and she'd right herself. How could she understand? Sometimes he was so tired. Every day he was treading water, and he wanted only to stop.

He took a cab from the airport straight to the Chicago office. Twenty-six miles east on the I-90 to Jackson and to Wacker and the cabbie listened to accordion music the whole way and never said a word. The meeting was in a conference room with views toward the water. It had already started when he got there. It had been going on all morning. There were white orchids on the table and stacks of tabbed papers. Danishes from breakfast with dried-out jelly centers. They argued about disclosure first and then Spellman wanted to know who'd pay the taxes. Ethan tried to explain how there wouldn't be any taxes, not the way this deal was structured, but Spellman was getting worked up. He scratched his bald head and pounded the table.

"Of course it matters," Spellman said. "You can't tell me for certain how things will go. Eight hundred dollars an hour and you're just guessing here," and Spellman's eyes popped the way those stress dolls do when you squeeze them. They needed some language to look at. They needed a draft tonight for their nine o'clock call. Hypothetical taxes and disregarded entities and Revenue Ruling 99-6. These things made him tired. Ethan moved his feet in circles beneath the table and kneaded the meat of his palms. All this sitting would give him a clot.

They took a break at two, and Ethan rolled his suitcase over to the hotel. The street was filled with construction crews. Men and a few women in yellow gear and muddy boots stood in line at the food trucks, and they ate hot dogs and gyro sandwiches standing up. A crew was laying rebar in the empty lot across the street. They tied it in places and walked along its length. Easy as gymnasts working the beam. It wasn't even thirty degrees out and the wind blew hard from the lake, but they didn't seem to mind. The buildings rose around them like cathedrals, and they were building another. It would last for two hundred years. He walked past them with his laptop and his suitcase, and all those winters in Colorado didn't prepare him for the wind. It was sharp as a blade how it worked its way through his coat. He pushed his collar up and kept on walking. Everywhere he looked there were cranes. Did they know how lucky they were? Those men who worked in concrete and steel and big slabs of marble. The welders and the bricklayers and the pipe insulation guys. They made things with their hands.

A group of kids walked past him with their teachers. On their way back from one of the museums probably. They wore name tags around their necks, and some of them carried pinwheels and held them high so the wind could turn them. They ran and pushed each other when the teachers weren't looking. The buses were waiting at the corner. The doors were already open, and the kids ran up the steps.

He set up his laptop when he got to the room. He unpacked his dress shirts and hung them in the bathroom. He turned the hot water on in the shower so the steam could work out some of the wrinkles. The room looked out onto a courtyard, and across the courtyard there was another tower with silver-colored windows. Seabirds flew over the buildings. They were probably five feet across with their wings open. Heading south to where the ocean was warm. The water wouldn't freeze where they were going. The air was always mild. He closed the curtains, and the room went dark. They kept out every trace of the afternoon sun. The room looked like every other room in the hotel, and the hotels all looked the same, too, from one city to the next.

He needed to look at the latest redline. They wanted the language before their call tonight. He should set up his alarm clocks before he forgot, but he was tired from the flight and from sitting in that room. He was tired from not exerting himself, and he lay back against the pillows. Ruby had packed his toiletries, and she'd set some butterscotch candies inside his bag because they were his favorite. He unwrapped a candy and then another. He fell asleep to that sweet taste.

It was warm in the city. The air was still and the water, too, and the moon touched everything with silver. She took him by the wrist. Her hair was wet and coiled down her bare shoulders. He heard crickets and frogs and the slapping sound of water. He knew the route. The black lava rocks and the trees and the sand where it curved. The stars in their strange patterns. *It's time*, the woman said. Her skin smelled like vinegar and roses. The girl was already there, just a little farther along the shore. Her face had no marks and her dress wasn't torn, and she moved with her mother's grace.

It was time to take the ferry. Time to go into that water and nothing would hurt him there. The wind would never blow. He took off his shoes and let the waves wash his feet. The woman squeezed his hand. He looked into those dark eyes, but he found no mercy there. She pulled, and he stayed where he was. Her grip was strong as any man's. No more winters where he was going. He could set his burdens down. A fisherman dragged his basket along the sand. It was full with octopus and strange curling things, and he beat them against the rocks. His arm stabbed downward through the air. All around them things were blooming and bursting and falling to rot. It smelled like Ruby's greenhouse. The woman pulled again, and her face was angry.

I'm sorry, Ethan said.

He needed to remember what he'd done. Ruby said he should remember it and make amends but set aside the pain. It was the seed and the pearl would grow around it, and he didn't deserve her. She talked to him sometimes just as he fell asleep. She whispered in his ear. *It won't happen from one day to the next.* It was a journey, and she said the same tired things that counselors everywhere said to drug addicts and gamblers and compulsive overeaters. *One step and then another.* Her fingers were gentle against his cheek.

The woman pulled harder, and Ethan pulled back. Her lips curled back from her teeth. He felt himself rising, and he didn't know why. Ficus trees grew in the city, and morning glories covered them. Everything was heavy with growing vines. He rose above these things. Above the water rolling against the sand. Rolling and falling back and he was over the treetops and he saw the woman and the girl farther down. Sweet girl walking into the water. God forgive him what he'd done. Above them and the fishermen tending their boats and the air was cool again and Ruby was calling his name. *Only you can save yourself,* Ruby always said, but she was wrong. She saved him every day. She saved him by singing in that lousy voice and by opening the blinds. Her voice pulled him upward, and he wasn't afraid. Above the city and its cathedrals. Above the sand and the dark water and he needed to thank her.

Halo

Mrs. Schrom wore a black halo the day before she died. Raymond saw it when she spiked her tomatoes out back and when she walked her dog. The next day her husband drove their horse trailer off the road. On Route 50 just past Gunnison. He lived because he was thrown from the truck, but Mrs. Schrom was wearing her seatbelt and she was strapped in tight. His mom told him not to draw any lessons from the accident. *You should always buckle up,* she said. Mrs. Schrom was the exception that proved the rule. Sister Mary Bee up the street wore a halo, too, but she was old and Raymond didn't notice at first. You had to watch carefully if you wanted to see them. They looked a lot like shadows.

The first time he saw one he reached for it, but his fingers went right through. His mom apologized. *He must like your hair,* she told old Mrs. Dreisser, who died the next day. She went to sleep and didn't wake up, and her daughter said it was a blessing. His mom had scolded him afterward. She shook her finger and said it wasn't nice to point, and Raymond knew then she couldn't see the things he saw.

He called the people angels though some of them were mean. They had halos, and they drove their cars and rolled past him in their wheelchairs. He saw them in shopping malls and in the hospital when his mom had her attack. It was her gallbladder. The doctors said it was filled with stones. She screamed until she was hoarse and the nurses all came running. Raymond waited in the hallway and covered up his ears, and the old man in the room next door had a halo over his bed. It hung in the air like a cloud. Like a swarm of honey bees. The next day the nurses changed the sheets in the old man's room. They stripped down his bed and rolled a new lady in, and that's when he started counting. He counted the floor tiles and the pictures in the hallway. He counted ambulances when they ran their sirens and the steps between her bathroom and the door, and all his counting made his mom well again. The numbers brought her home.

How many peas were on his plate and how many birds sitting on the wire and he counted them while they flew. There was magic in them. He knew this without anyone saying so. The magic would keep his dad's plane from crashing. He was a pilot for Continental and gone three days a week. The food was cold by the time Raymond finished his counting. Sometimes he lost track and had to begin again. His mom didn't understand why he took so long to eat. "Something's not right with you," she said. "Don't be like your Aunt Leslie. Twenty years of counseling and she still can't eat a cookie." He pushed his food around when she started to worry. He took a forkful of peas and counted them against his tongue and she looked happy then. She relaxed a little and smiled, and she didn't know he was keeping score. He was holding up heaven with his numbers. He was keeping the halos away.

His Grandma Hooper knew her angels. Michael and Raphael the healer and Uriel who stands by people just before they die. She had angel heads on her wall and pictures of Saint George killing the serpent. Raymond sat with her because his mom was at the gym. They watched TV together even though her eyes were bad. She couldn't read her magazines anymore or her mystery books, but she didn't want cataract surgery either because those doctors could mess you up. She knew a lady whose eyelids started drooping the day after the surgeons cut her. Her friend's eyes were clear now, but what good did it do if she couldn't keep them open.

His grandma made him grilled cheese sandwiches with extra butter. She made caramel corn in the microwave, and they ate together from the bowl. They watched *Touched by an Angel* and *Highway to Heaven.* Thank God for those reruns and for Lawrence Welk, she said. She didn't like violence in her house. She didn't allow cuss words either because bad thoughts leave traces. If they linger they become a sin. "Fix your mind on righteous things," she told him, and her eyes were gray and bright.

There were clouds on the TV, and the angel was walking along the road. He was in the desert where there weren't any people. It was his job to help people so he could earn his wings. Look how nice TV used to be, she was saying. It used to lift us up. It wasn't like it is now with all those naked ladies. You can't go half an hour without seeing something bad. Raymond nodded though he didn't know exactly what she meant. He reached for the popcorn bowl she held on her knee.

"I see angels sometimes," he said. "I see them with their halos."

His grandma scratched her chin. Her fingers were bent from her years in the shoe store. She talked about it sometimes. All the orthopedic shoes she sold to women with hammer toes and bunions.

"Their halos are black," Raymond said.

His grandma looked at him now. "We don't talk about those," she said, but her voice wasn't angry. She reached for the remote and turned the volume up. "They're traveling, and we leave them alone."

He washed the bowl for her once her shows were done, and he pulled the weeds from her gravel beds. She used gasoline sometimes, too, but the neighbors didn't like it. She sat on the porch with a sweating can of Sprite. "You're a good boy," she called out when he tossed the weeds into the bin and rolled it to the curb. "Come sit with me before you burn." She was careful with the sun because that's what killed Grandpa Hooper. It started with a spot at the top of his head. Just a single brown spot that set down roots and spread.

Raymond sat beside her on the bench, and she patted his sweaty head. "I used to have hair just as red as yours," she said. "It was what your grandpa noticed first." It skipped a generation with his momma, she was saying. She got the German and not the Irish with that straight blond hair she had. They watched the sun set behind the mountains, and she looked right at it with her cloudy eyes and she didn't blink or shade herself. He wanted to ask her more about the angels. He wanted to ask her where they were going, but he already knew.

•

On Friday afternoons he and his mom went to Leon Gessi's to share a pepperoni pizza. She said carbs were okay once a week. That's why she took those spinning classes and lifted all those weights. They were early today. They went at three o'clock and not at five, and most of the high school students were still waiting for their slices. They clustered around the foosball table and some ancient video games. The boys and girls dressed alike. They wore tight jeans and black nail polish, and their skin was so white he could see the veins around their eyes. They looked like spirits, those high school kids. They looked like the anime his parents wouldn't let him watch. A group of them pushed by, three boys and two girls with pale pale eyes. They carried greasy plates and cans of soda pop. They laughed as they went out, and they wore halos, all of them. He watched them climb into a dented old car. It was rusted through in places. They pulled into the street so fast the tires left long marks and another car honked at them and had to hit the brakes.

Two weeks since his dad had been gone. Two weeks and three days, and Raymond sorted his Legos by color and grouped them in batches of ten. He counted the paper clips his dad kept in a jar. The pennies in the kitchen and the bolts and screws on his dad's workbench. He wrote the numbers down, one after the next, and the lists kept getting longer. He piled them on his floor and taped them to his headboard. He went outside, too, behind the compost heap where the crickets had built a nest. Some were as long as his pinkie, and their backs were spotted with green and gold. All their moving made it hard to count them, and so he took his mom's garden shoes and crushed them one by one. He made them beautiful while he counted them. He set them out like sun rays over the patio stones.

His mom shouted when she saw them. She dropped her laundry basket. "What's wrong with you?" She pulled him up and into the house. She looked scared like when she had to brake the car too fast and she'd throw her arm across his chest. They went together to his room, and she opened up the blinds. "Why don't you play like the other kids? Why don't you ride your bike anymore or play video games at Ryan's?"

He sat on his bed and watched her walk back and forth across the room, from his desk to his sliding closet doors. She stopped beside his bed. She pulled the lists off the headboard. "What are these?" She waved the papers in the air. She'd probably seen them a hundred times before, when she made his bed each morning and when she ran the vacuum, but she noticed them only now. "What's all this stuff you keep writing?" She brought the papers to the window and looked at them in the sunlight. She squinted a little because she didn't have her glasses, and for the first time he noticed how she looked like his Grandma Hooper. Not her hair but the lines in her forehead and how she worked her jaw.

"What are these numbers?" She waved the papers again as if they'd talk to her if she shook them hard enough. "What do they mean?"

Raymond shifted on his bed. There were some birds in the plum tree just outside his window. They sat in a perfect line. It looked like five of them, but there might be more if he could only see them. "I'm just counting," he said. "I'm counting them before they go away."

She sat beside him on the bed and put her arm around his shoulders. "Nobody's going away," she said. "I'm right here, and your dad's coming home in another week. He just needs a little time." She gathered up all the papers from his desk and from under his bed. She even found the ones he'd taped inside his closet doors. She started talking about how eleven was a difficult age and sometimes even the good kids needed a little help. She took his lists away. She clipped them together and didn't tell him where she'd put them, but it didn't matter. As soon as she'd left he opened his notebook and started a new one.

His therapist Dr. Winer had thirty-seven snow globes. Her husband brought them back from all his business trips, and she bought her own, too, when they went together on vacation. She had dancing hula girls from when they went to Hawaii and snow angels from Vienna. The Golden Gate Bridge in San Francisco—the prettiest city in the country, Dr. Winer said, if you can stand the fog—and a stern-looking Lincoln sitting in his chair. She had a mermaid, too, with white blond hair streaming upward in the water. Her eyes were closed, and there were golden flowers behind her ears. Dr. Winer kept them on a ledge just below her window, and on sunny days Raymond liked to shake them and watch the glitter settle.

Dr. Winer's face had no wrinkles, not a single line, but her hair was mostly silver. She wore it loose, and it made her look young and old at once. She listened closely when he talked. She wanted to know about school and how often his dad was gone. He talked about his counting sometimes but not in ways she'd understand. He couldn't tell her how it was a relief and how it kept away the halos. She wanted to know why he'd killed all those crickets. "Why did you spread them on the sidewalk?" She looked at him the way his mom did when she was worried. She wrinkled up her forehead, and the sun came through the window and lit up her gray hair.

"I was praying," he told her. And he didn't know why he said it or exactly what it meant, but it was true. True the way dreams are or tears when you're hurt. He was praying for the people with halos and those who were still waiting.

His mom was proud of how he was acting. "You're calmer than you were before," she said. "You're not tapping the way you used to or playing with your food." She was wearing a sweatshirt from the gym and her Adidas running shoes. She exercised every day now and not just at the gym. She watched the fitness shows in the morning and bought a purple yoga mat. She did sit-ups on a rubber ball and old-fashioned push-ups and jumping jacks. "This is the way your Grandpa Hooper did it when he was in the army," she said. "I never saw a man who could do so many push-ups." Raymond helped her count when she got tired. He kept track of all the numbers.

She wiped her forehead when she was done and drank from her bottle of vitamin water. "All you needed was somebody who could listen," she said. "A professional and not just me or your Grandma Hooper." She screwed the cap back on and set the bottle down. "She's gotten strange since your grandpa died. It's all that time alone."

His mom was looking at him, and her eyes were serious. She was waiting for him to agree, but she was wrong about the doctor and about his grandma, too. "Grandma's not alone," he said. "Every week I go to see her." Her eyes were full with angels and spirits, he wanted to say. How could she be lonely when she wasn't ever alone.

Dr. Winer said people need space to breathe. That was true for grown-ups like his parents and it was true for kids, too. She asked him if he thought the numbers were keeping him from making friends. Maybe he spent too much time alone when he should be playing instead. She was wrong, of course, but he didn't mind. He liked the sound of her voice and the way the light came through her office window. There was a courtyard two floors down and a maple tree that had started to flower. Another month and the choppers would fall from the branches. Those seeds would flutter down like wings. All that time he spent in Dr. Winer's office, all that time talking and watching the branches through the window, and this is what he learned: It's good to have somebody who will listen even if they don't understand.

Count the tiles in the bathroom floor, but not the cracked one by the tub. That one brought bad luck. The cans in the pantry and the empty water bottles. His mother never stacked them right. She piled them by the washer. Count them and carry the numbers with you because you'll need them where you're going. Mr. Driscoll the school bus driver coughed six times before they got to Chelton. He had asthma this time of year. He said it was the pollen. Count them and keep them and work them round and round until they give him back his air.

He cleaned out his Grandma Hooper's gutters. It was May already, and she was worried about rain. She let him climb the ladder and walk along the roof. There were needles up there and bent rusty nails, and he felt like his dad when he stood on those shingles. He was flying in the clouds. Grandma Hooper looked so small down there. She was wearing her jogging pants and her VFW visor. "Be careful at the edges," she was saying. "Take it slow and steady." He gathered up the leaves and all the needles and stuffed them in a garbage bag. By the time he was halfway around the house the bag was full to bursting. He found a dead raccoon and a bird's nest with cracked pieces of pale green shell. He wondered where the birds had gone and whether the babies had lived. He'd seen a blue jay once eat a baby starling. It lifted the baby right from the nest and carried it away. "Tie it up," his grandma said. Her hands were on her hips. "Drop it down when it's full."

He'd filled up two bags and started a third before he was done. He went back down the ladder, and that was worse than climbing up. He couldn't see where he was going. His grandma dusted him off and made him wipe his shoes, and she had the ice cream ready. She'd let it get a little soft so she could work the scooper. "Don't tell your momma what you did for me," she said. "I don't want her to worry. And don't tell her about the ice cream either. She's fussy when it comes to sugar."

"I won't tell," he said. His mom had too many worries already, and they were mostly about him.

He ate his ice cream, stirring it around until it was smooth as pudding, and his grandma started to pray. She prayed when the mood hit her because she didn't believe in churches. She set her hands together and talked directly to the king of kings. The one who knows things that are uncertain and obscure. "Grant me strength," she said, "and bless my babies all of them and the travelers far from home." Her voice went deep, and her eyes were closed so she could feel the spirit.

She kissed him on the cheek when his mom came to pick him up. Her lips were dry as paper. She leaned in close and held him by the shoulders, and her hands were stronger than they looked. "Don't be scared," she said. "Show them kindness while they're here."

Four weeks and six days and eleven hours. The numbers didn't bring his father home. Forty-nine thousand six hundred and twenty minutes. It was longer than he'd ever been gone before, and his mom was on the LifeCycle again. She'd stopped putting on her lipstick and blow-drying her hair. She worked out until her face was shiny. "One thing in this life is true as the stars," she said. "Your daddy and I both love you."

•

Dr. Winer wasn't sitting in her chair when he came in to see her. She was underneath her desk. "I've lost my earring," she was saying. "I heard it when it fell." She was moving around down there, and Raymond went on his knees, too, so he could help her look. He crawled on the outside of the desk and felt the wood floor with his fingers.

"I've got the backing right here," she said. "But I can't find the pearl."

Raymond worked his way in circles away from the desk. The sun was coming through the window, and it shone across the wooden floors and made them look like honey. He was halfway to the wall before he found the earring. It was gold and not white like the pearls his mom put on when she wore her party dress.

"I've got it," he said. He pushed himself up and held it high so she could see it was okay. "Look how far it rolled."

Doctor Winer came up from behind her desk. She smiled and pulled her sweater straight, and everything about her was touched with silver. Raymond had to cover his eyes. "You saved me today," she said, and she came to him and took it from his hand. "My husband bought me these on our honeymoon."

She stepped out from the light. She put the earring back in her ear and checked to make sure it was in tight, and when she turned around there was a shadow over her head. Raymond saw it floating in the air. It was real as the pearl he'd found or the scabs on his hands from cleaning his grandma's gutters.

"We're going to the Bahamas next week," Dr. Winer said. She rolled her chair back to its spot, and the halo went with her. "I want to take this pair along."

She sat down the way she always did, and she reached for her pen and notebook. "Three months taking lessons in a pool, and I'll finally see some fish."

Raymond looked out the window. The gardeners were wheeling the mowers off their truck. The lawn was green already, and they'd started planting the flower beds. "Look how nice it is out there," he said. "It's warm enough for shorts." He could hear the halo this time.

It was thrumming like a hive. The sound filled the room, and the doctor didn't notice. "Are you sure you have to go?"

"It won't be long. Not even two weeks."

Raymond didn't sit down in his chair. He went to the window where she kept her snow globes and picked up the sleeping mermaid. He cradled her in his hand. She sat beside a treasure chest, and there were stones inside and strands of silver pearls.

He shook the globe and set it back down. He leaned over the window ledge. Three of the gardeners were gathered around the fountain. They were wet from working the nozzle. One of them had a metal brush, and he was scrubbing down the cement and the tiles around the basin. The water made a rainbow in the sun. They were working beneath it and didn't look up, but Raymond saw it from where he was. He saw the droplets and the birds in the branches. He saw every tile and tree.

"Maybe you shouldn't go." He wanted to tell her that he saw bad things sometimes. That he knew what was going to happen. She should stay where she was because it was almost summer. The air was sweet, but the mountains still had their snow. "My mom says people fall off those cruise ships."

"That's true," Dr. Winer said. "But people can fall at home, too. And we're just going on a little sailboat. Even if I fall they'll turn around and find me." It was beautiful where she was going, she told him. The water was bathtub-warm.

She turned serious again and started to ask him questions. She wanted to know about things that weren't important. His dad was flying planes from Denver to Phoenix and staying in a hotel. His mom was working out more every day, and the veins were starting to show in her arms. All those sets he counted and her face was clenched from the strain and she didn't look stronger when she was done. The exercise was wearing her down.

He walked back and forth behind Dr. Winer's desk. He could hear her pen pushing against the paper, and he didn't look at her or the cloud over her head. Her computer was humming and the halo, too, and he wanted to cover his ears. It'd be a blessing if his eyes went cloudy. He could go outside then. He wouldn't have to look at the ground. He'd pray for people he couldn't see, and he wouldn't feel their passing.

His mother rang the office bell before the hour was over. Her watch was always a little fast. Dr. Winer stood up at the sound. She went to the window and picked up the mermaid. "Keep her," she said. "This one's always been your favorite. I could tell from the first day you came."

She set it in his hands. Before he could say no or give it back, she pulled him in for a hug. She hadn't done that before, and he held on to her and didn't let go, not until his mother came through the door.

Sea of Tranquility

It began with a shimmering in both his eyes. He was sitting at the store monitor and the letters started to blur. They went from black to silver, and he rubbed his eyes and closed the shades to cut down on the glare. It was almost six o'clock in the evening and he needed to check the database tables. They were liquidating the inventory, but nobody was buying. A lady had come in at lunchtime and napped on the Tempurpedic without any explanation. She thanked him when she left and straightened out her skirt. Couples came in all day long and bickered because the mattresses were too hard or too soft or weren't suitable for backsleepers. He was thankful for Marci then because she didn't fuss about the little things. She'd stopped coloring her hair, but she still drank wine at dinner. *Fetuses need antioxidants, too,* she'd say. *It's my duty to eat chocolate.*

He scrolled through the summary table which showed him every mattress left in the store and down at the warehouse on Cascade. He'd switched the store to IntelliTrack because that program really worked, but he couldn't stay focused now because the numbers were silver and the monitor, too, and it was like looking at snow with the sun shining on it.

The bell on the door rang and it was a blond lady with an Alaskan husky on a leash. Even from across the showroom he could see the dog's pale eyes. The lady's eyes were blue, too, and rimmed with dark liner. She was dressed like a teenager with her skinny jeans, but she must have been over sixty. "I'm sorry, ma'am," he said. "Unless that's a service dog you can't bring him inside."

The lady sat down on the Serta Perfect Day right beside the door. The dog jumped up beside her, and they lay down together like a man and wife. "He's not hurting anybody," she said. Her voice was young, too, almost high-pitched as a girl's. She looked up at the ceiling and set her hands behind her head.

"That's true," he said. As he came closer to the Serta their faces began to blur. He saw only their outlines and the blue of her jeans and jacket. "But I can't have dogs sleeping on our samples."

She sat up and he couldn't see the expression on her face or whether her eyes were open, but he saw her hand come to her hip like a schoolteacher lecturing a wayward student. "How are we supposed to know if it's comfortable if we both can't try it out?"

"Why don't you tie him up out front? That way you can take your time."

"That won't work," she said. "We make all our decisions together."

"I'm sorry," he said again, and he held out both his hands. "I don't think I can help you." They always came in just before closing. The cranky people with herniated discs and the peculiar folks with their Burger King bags who wanted to eat their french fries on his samples.

"Don't tell me you're sorry," she said. "I hear that every day. Where's your manager? I need to talk to him."

"I'm the manager. I manage all our stores in town." He looked back at the clock over the desk and it was quarter past six. Another fifteen minutes and he could lock the door.

"No wonder you're going out of business. With policies like that." She stood up and her dog did, too, and he held the door for them and watched them walk past the liquor store and the Summit eco-cleaners. He could see them clearly once they were farther away. She turned one more time to look back at his store, and he could tell from her profile she'd once been pretty.

He went to Walgreens and bought reading glasses like the ones his father used to wear. Little Ben Franklin lenses that sat low on his nose. He started with the 1.5 power glasses because the stronger ones made him dizzy. He had a pair in the bathroom so he could read his science magazines and another on his nightstand. He had three more pairs at the store. For a little while when he wore them the clouds were gone from his eyes, and he could read the sheets again and update the database entries. Marci teased him because he left them everywhere. *Hey, grandpa,* she'd say. *All you need is a sweater vest and a pipe,* and she'd give him a light punch in the ribs because she knew he couldn't hit her back. She stood there in her nurse's scrubs and he could see her face again and the pooch of her belly. She was three months along and just beginning to show. Every morning she looked a little different.

On Saturdays he left early to go running. He got up without turning on the lights because Marci needed her sleep. She tossed at night even with her earplugs. She said it was her hormones, she could feel them bubbling in her blood, and then she'd laugh because nurses weren't supposed to talk that way.

He went to Garden of the Gods because he didn't mind the tourists. The loop took him past the Twin Sisters rock formation and the gift shop parking lot and up a narrow trail. The rocks were beside him and he saw them as blurs of red, but he couldn't make out the sandy spots or the ruts left by the horses. Past the first and second parts and up the railroad ties that terraced the hill for riding. He knew these steps and how to climb them, and he wasn't sure if he was seeing them now or running them from memory. Past those steps the trail turned south and went across the ridge. He stopped at the top and leaned against a boulder. He drank from his water bottle.

There were no trees where he was and no other hills to block his view. The wind had started blowing, and it was hot as a hairdryer how it came through the junipers. It turned his sweat to salt. Marci should be here with him because she liked those summer breezes. She was a cactus and not a fern, that's what she always said. She could never live in one of those mossy states the way her sisters did. The road just below him was getting crowded. Silhouettes of people pushing their strollers and riding recumbent bikes. Flashes of color against the rocks. He could see every ripple in the distance, every shadow and groove and all the pitons and eyebolts left by climbers before the regulations got too strict. He'd been coming here since he was a kid, but he'd never noticed these things before. How the cumulus clouds weren't just white. They had purple in them and silver. A prairie falcon circled the road half a mile away, riding the thermals above the asphalt. He saw the yellow of its talons and its russet marble eye. It had hairs around the holes in its beak, which caught him by surprise. They were fine as a cat's whiskers. Everything was so clear it almost hurt to look. The garter snakes far down in the grasses and the frogs with their camouflage skin, the tiny mushroom of red dust left by a jackrabbit as it hopped. This is what it felt like to be an eagle or an angel. To see things as if he'd designed them himself and knew all their inner workings.

He bought new reading glasses with a higher magnification. The kind the really old folks use, 1.75, then 2.5 and finally 3.5, and that was as high as the Walgreens inventory went, but even with the strongest pair, he could see only the outline of his hands. He couldn't see the hairs on his wrist or his veins or whether his nails were dirty. He needed an enormous lens in front of his computer monitor just to read his e-mails. He made an appointment with the optometrist for Thursday in four weeks. They could see him earlier if it was an emergency, but he told them no, it was nothing urgent. Both his parents had worn glasses and he was just getting old.

The moon had terraces in its craters, giant steps of lava rock. There was a deep basin in the upper half and mountains like jagged teeth. In the moon's first quarter three more craters appeared along the crescent where it went dark. He thought of them as sisters, and sometimes they glowed white at their centers as if they were boiling over. The fourth quarter brought a lake, bigger than all the others, with a white streak down its middle like a lightning bolt. Thumbprints and nipples and chickenpox scars. Veins running just below the surface. He stood by the front window while Marci was sleeping and mapped all the ridges and peaks. One night he tried to draw the things he saw. He took a pencil and a pad, but when he sat down at the kitchen table, he couldn't focus on the paper clearly, not even with his glasses.

He was locking up the store when everything went black. It was a Friday at half past six. He knelt down by the door with his key, and the darkness took him by surprise and made him lose his balance. It felt like an eclipse at first or a complete electrical failure. Like black velvet curtains falling over a stage. Outside the glass door the liquor store was gone and the Korean BBQ at the corner. There were no cars, no parking lot or dumpsters or stop signs. Everything he knew was gone except for a stretch of cloudless sky. He crawled the length of the store, feeling his way along the carpet tiles until he got back to his desk. That's where he stayed until Marci came to get him.

He held on to her sleeve the whole way to the hospital. He saw only the blue sky and the mountains, but not the dashboard or her face. He clutched her hand so tight he was afraid he would hurt her, but she didn't pull away. She kept saying he shouldn't panic. There was an explanation and the doctors would figure it out. The ophthalmologists at Memorial were some of the best ones in the state. *Maybe it's hysterical blindness,* she was saying. It could be all the stress from closing down the store, or it might be an ocular migraine or a transient episode in his brain. *These things happen. They happen all the time,* and he wanted to believe her.

They tested him for glaucoma and occlusions in his internal carotid artery. They checked his retinas for cholesterol crystals and made sure they hadn't detached, but everything looked normal. They injected dye into his arm next and photographed the inside of his eye to see if the veins were leaking, and the doctors stood around his chair and talked about him as if he were a textbook case and not a living patient. Nurses rolled him around the hallways and he could hear ventilators in places and the beeping of machines, snatches of voices he hadn't heard before, but they all were somehow familiar. The MRI technician sounded like a smoker. She coughed just like his Uncle Lewis who'd died from emphysema. She set the line with the contrast dye into his forearm, and it burned when it went in. "Keep your eyes closed," she said. "That always makes it better."

The CT scans came next. Then the specialists from Denver who ignored him when he said he could see things in the distance. "Let's go outside," he told them, "and I'll show you what I mean," but they talked only about his ocular fundus and his arterial branches. One of the doctors asked him if he was a veteran or had experienced any recent psychological trauma. He said he could be converting his stress into vision failure. Another doctor named Mitkoff was convinced there was a neurological reason. "Your pupils have decreased constriction," he said. "They don't respond normally to the light. The things you see are only illusions." There was a name for this syndrome where the blind had beautiful visions. They saw butterflies and songbirds and climbing lattice patterns, and what could he say to these experts who were so certain they were right.

On the seventh day the doctors still couldn't agree. They discharged him with referrals to a psychiatrist and the Wilmer Eye Institute at Johns Hopkins. Marci left her shift early and rolled him through the doors. He didn't want to use the chair, but she said it was hospital policy. He couldn't see the parking lot or the sliding glass doors at the hospital entrance. He couldn't see her hands on the wheelchair handles, but just before they got to the car he looked up at the sky. The moon was full and it was hanging there and he saw all its familiar craters. Normally he needed the crescent to make out the details because that's when the sun threw the strongest shadows, but he saw the ripples now and every swirling cloud.

It wasn't eight o'clock yet, and the sky was halfway between blue and black. He followed its dome downward and there were the distant mountains he'd seen every day of his life. The mountains and the lights along the hills and those matchstick houses on the eastern plains with all their windows lit. The red taillights two miles away on Academy streaking northward through the city. Things began in shadow and got sharper as they receded. There was an enormous circle of blackness around him, he understood this now. It was big as an ocean and getting bigger, and it followed him where he went.

•

In the fall of 1961 something knocked a Soviet spacecraft off its orbit. He'd read about this when he was little. There were three cosmonauts inside, though even now the Russians will deny it. You can listen to the tapes if you know how to find them. An Italian monitoring station caught the final exchanges when the cosmonauts asked for help. You can hear their breathing over the static. One of them was praying and it sounded like a song, but they drifted outward and nobody could bring them back and nobody ever tried. What did that last surviving cosmonaut see as he floated into space? The books won't tell us that. Four hundred thirty miles from earth but no closer to the stars.

She set his hand on her belly. It was only September, but the nights were already crisp. They were together in Old Farm Park just behind the silo, and the grade wasn't steep but she'd huffed when she led him up the hill. "If I get any bigger, they'll need a forklift to move me," she said. "They'll need one of those piano cranes." He'd set his jacket down on the concrete bench so she wouldn't be too cold. Sitting on cold stone wasn't good for the baby, he'd learned this from his mother. She worked his hand in circles and he could feel her belly button through the wool of her sweater. It stuck out like a little thumb.

He forgot he lived in the city on nights like these. Sometimes he heard owls calling or the crash of the dumpsters by the country club where the coyotes dug for scraps. The city was full of creatures. She leaned against his shoulder the way she used to when they went to the movies. She was breathing a little quickly now that she was seven months along. Everything about her went a little faster. Her stomach gurgled even if all she ate was crackers. She called it bubble gut.

On walks like this she'd tell him he'd waited long enough. He needed to make an appointment with those folks at Johns Hopkins. She knew the doctors by name and where they went to school. They could go together once the baby was born. They could try some of those famous crabcakes. But tonight she leaned a little closer, and he could feel her breath against his ear. "You be my telescope for a while," she said. "Tell me what you see."

He took her hand, and for once it was warmer than his. He latticed his fingers into hers. He told her about the lake on the right side of the moon and how it was shaped like a maple leaf. That was where the astronauts had landed the year that he was born. They'd left their bootprints in that gray powder. He told her about Mars and the mountain at its center. It looked big as Everest from where he sat. It cast an enormous shadow. The canyons in every direction and the pitted plains and the trails that wound between the rocks like mining roads in the desert. *Look how beautiful it is,* he wanted to tell her. *Somebody made these things. Nothing here is accidental.*

Her breathing got a little deeper while he talked. It sounded like she was beginning to doze. He shifted on the bench, careful not to wake her. There were satellites flashing just above the horizon, strange iridium flares and slowly moving devices. He counted eleven just while he was sitting there, propellers and wagon wheels and one of them was like an enormous biplane with four rotating arms. The sky was busy as an interstate. Who knew why there weren't more crashes.

He qualified for Social Security, but he didn't want to take it. His vision was worse than 2/200 and his visual field was less than twenty degrees, and either one alone would be enough to get him benefits. "You've earned that money," Marci said. "You've paid into the system and now you get some back." The company's regional manager up in Denver told him the same thing. "There's always a place for you here," he said. "But take care of yourself first because your health is all that matters." All the things people told each other in times of trouble, and what good did they do? He was useless sitting there with his coffee mug while Marci worked the cordless drill and put the crib together. She kept dropping those little screws. "Crap," she'd say, "crap there goes another one," and it was hard for her to bend down and fish them off the carpet. "If it takes all night I'm putting this thing together." She laughed a little when she said it. She wasn't even three feet away, but he was lonely sitting beside her.

The Shamrock sign was gone and the lights on Stetson Hills. The maple trees by Prospect Park that had started turning early. His blindness was rippling outward. It took away his city one piece at a time. The closest mountains had started to blur as if someone had smudged their edges with an eraser. They'd go away one day. He'd wake up and they'd be gone, and he wondered if he'd miss them.

The first few hours of labor she watched the soaps. He called her sisters in Seattle to tell them the good news. He stood behind the sofa and rubbed her shoulders when she got tired from the pacing. She told him what the actors were wearing and who was sleeping together. Jason was back on *General Hospital*, she was saying, but he wasn't with Liz now because his loyalties were with the mob. Luke was still on the show and he was looking a little ragged. Some sunscreen would have made all the difference there. She didn't stop talking, not even when the contractions came. "They're no worse than a period cramp," she said. "It's nothing I can't handle," but by the time the cab pulled up her voice had started to tremble.

It was like a submarine in the delivery room with all the monitors humming. The room felt pressurized, and every three minutes Marci started to moan. She squeezed her fingers around his hand so tight the bones shifted in his wrist. This was the moment they'd been waiting for since she showed him the pregnancy stick, but now that it was here it sounded like an exorcism and not their baby's birth. He held on to the metal bed rail in case she tried to choke him. "God damn," she said. "It's not supposed to hurt this bad," and he kissed the sweaty crown of her head. Her *Magic of the Earth* CD was playing in the background. An endless loop of whales and rainshowers and breaking ocean waves.

Seven hours later she was still at five centimeters and the nurses started the Pitocin drip. He tried to wipe her brow with a washcloth, but he banged against her nose instead. After that he was afraid to touch her because he might mess up the needles. She was panting like somebody passing a stone, but she wasn't opening the way she should. They upped the Pitocin two times in the next three hours, and she really started to shout then. Things began to happen. People gathered around her bed. It felt like a dozen people from all their voices. The room was tight as an elevator caught between two floors.

A nurse was telling Marci when to push and she talked like a drill sergeant or a football coach. "Now's the time," she kept saying. "Give it all you've got."

He felt a strange tightness inside his chest when Marci gasped for air, as if he couldn't breathe unless she did. The tightness worked its way up into his throat. "Yes," people were saying. "That's right. You're doing great," and all those voices were jumbled together with the sound of falling rain. He held his breath without meaning to, and he didn't exhale until he heard his son screaming in the room.

He weighed six pounds eleven ounces exactly. The drill sergeant said he was nineteen and one half inches long. "He's got a good pair of lungs," she told them. "You've got yourself a screamer." Marci held him first, and she kept him for the longest time. The nurse told her to smile so she could take a picture. "You, too, daddy," she said. "Get a little closer to the bed." She took three pictures and he wasn't sure where to look, and when the nurse was done Marci took their boy and set him in his arms.

"Don't be afraid," she said. "He looks like you. He's got your nose exactly."

His son squirmed against his elbow. He worked his legs like a turtle flipped on its back, and this was as light as he'd ever be. A clumsy moment and they could lose him. He might drop his boy on the hard floor if his attention wandered. He might bump him against a doorframe or a wall. He ran his thumb over that waxy newborn skin, but his hands weren't sensitive the way blind people's were supposed to be. There wasn't anything distinctive about that bald head. This baby could belong to anyone. The doctors could switch one for the other, and he would never know.

The cloudy days were hardest. The nights when the baby cried, all those starless nights when Marci ran to feed him. *You can't just sit there forever,* she'd say. The house smelled like diapers and burnt baby formula, and he should have tried to help her. He should have found a way, but he just sat there like a train passenger and looked outside his window. He was waiting, and she wouldn't understand this. He was waiting for the winds to come and give him back his sky.

•

The highest mountain on Mars had a crater at its center. It had streaks of red and gray. The black sand dunes and the clifftops and the places where the rocks had slid a million years before. A dust storm turning over the planet's surface and its center made a perfect T. Be grateful for these things. They will get clearer before they go away. He recognized Saturn from his childhood books, but there were other ones, too, with copper-colored haloes and he didn't know their names. He saw dragonfly wings and a teapot constellation with clouds of violet steam. He saw his father's eyes.

They drove together along Austin Bluffs and she wouldn't tell him why. All she'd say was that they were going back to school. "Back to the scene of the crime," she said. "When I was skinny and you still had all your hair." She unfolded one of their camping chairs once they got to the visitors' lot. She set two hand warmers in his pockets and a travel mug with instant cocoa in the cup rest on his right.

"Can you see the scar?" She turned his chin toward the mountain where the limestone quarry used to be. Fifteen or twenty miles, maybe a little more. It was far enough away for him to see it clearly. The county was years into the reclamation but there weren't any trees yet, just milkweed and prickly pear and tufts of frozen grasses. "That's where you need to look."

"Jesus, Marci. All that's out there is some sheep."

"I'll call you when I'm ready." She kissed him on the temple and wiped away the spit. "And don't complain about the wind. It's the warmest it's been all week."

He heard the car as she drove away. A Camry she'd had since '98, but she always mashed the gears. Some students were laughing in the courtyard just behind the lot. It wasn't a commuter school anymore. The last time he'd driven by there'd been real dormitories laid out in a grid and not just a few scattered buildings. The cafeteria was probably gone where he and Marci used to sit fifteen years before. Anthropology and statistics and introductory accounting, he raced up the hill three nights a week and what did he remember? Early man used oldowan tools to get the marrow out of bones. The australopithecenes could break rocks with their jaws. He still had his lecture notes in a plastic box next to the water heater.

"Sir." A girl touched his shoulder. She knelt down beside him and spoke loudly in his ear, as if he were deaf and not just blind. "Sir, are you alright? Are you waiting for a ride?"

"I'm bird-watching," he told her. "I'm looking for big-horns up in the hills." The girl stepped back then, and the people with her laughed. After that they left him alone.

He dozed a little in the sun. He drank some of his cocoa. A football game was playing on somebody's TV. Somebody else was listening to a Spanish language tape in one of the buildings behind the lot. *Soy Antonio García Morales,* a man said. *Yo soy chileno. De dónde eres tú,* but the window closed before anyone could answer. Snatches of laughter and conversation and the voices all sounded so young. Marci was right, he knew this. He needed to see an occupational therapist so he could get his bearings. He needed to send in his Social Security papers and make an appointment at Johns Hopkins. But not today and not tomorrow either. All these things could wait. The sky would be clear tonight, and he'd see all his familiar places.

Two hours later give or take the car came into focus. He saw it before she called. It was working its way up the red dirt road that wound across the mountain. She'd scraped the fender sometime in the last few months, and the green paint had started to blister. It looked almost matte in the sun, like the Humvees the soldiers drove between Fort Carson and the city. She parked right below the quarry gate and stepped out from the car. She wore a knit hat he hadn't seen before. She frowned right at him as if she could see him sitting in his chair.

She opened the back door and bent down by the car seat. When she turned around she had their boy cradled against her shoulder. He was bundled up in a yellow parka like the Stay Puft man. She took off his cap and set it in her coat pocket. His fists were clenched against the cold. His hair was pale as corn silk. The January sun was shining but it threw off no warmth and she was holding up their boy. She raised him like a banner.

Weights and Measures

T he nest fell from the eaves and landed below his window. The guys from All Year Gutters were up there walking on the shingles. Every summer they came, and they weren't careful with their hoses. They hit his balcony and his mountain bike, and it didn't matter if he complained. The president of the condo board was always somewhere else. Playing golf in Arizona or fishing in Cancún, and he didn't stop to listen when Jason caught him between trips. He just waved and kept on going. *Where's that pretty wife of yours,* he'd say. *It's been ages since I've seen her.* Jason hated him even more then. Not even fifty and retired already. Always smiling and always wearing shiny leather shoes. Tan as a politician and he went to a salon where the ladies buffed his nails.

He went outside though the workmen were still spraying the water. They were shouting over the thump of the compressor. The birds were wet and their skin was dimpled gray and they were dead, all of them, except for one still in the nest. They looked like tiny ducklings. Like plucked birds hanging from hooks the way he'd seen in San Francisco. They'd gone to Chinatown there just after they were married. They'd walked together on those narrow streets, and Shelby bought straw hats and umbrellas made of paper and a tiny painted tea set for when they had a daughter.

He knelt on the wet concrete so he could see it better. It lay curled on its stomach like a baby in a cradle. Its eyes were closed, and he reached for it. Not even a trace yet of feathers. It was a tiny thing no bigger than his pinkie. It was a heartbeat in his palm. He was scared a little the way he always was when he touched something wild.

His duffel bag was packed already and waiting at the door. He was supposed to be in Guffy where she was waiting at the cabin. Sixty miles west on the 24 past the fossil beds, past the Eleven Mile Reservoir where they'd camped together on their honeymoon. He'd taken ten vacation days, and they'd go on the trails the way they used to. They'd pick the first raspberries. She said it was important to find a happy spot. Not the condo where they'd spent the last eight years and not her new place either. She was staying out in Rockrimmon with some Christian Scientists, and none of it made sense. A pharmacist living with folks who think disease is an illusion. They didn't vaccinate their kids against the measles or take penicillin if they were infected. She'd taken their beagle Lucy and the stationary bike, and she cried sometimes when she called. She asked him if he missed her.

He built a nest of white socks on the coffee table. He filled the hot-water bottle and wrapped it in a towel. His mother had raised sparrows and gray-crowned rosy finches. She dusted them for mites and kept them in the kitchen. *There's nothing sweeter*, she'd say, *than a baby starling when it sleeps.* She taught him how to wet their beaks and how to mix their food. Dog food worked, or cat food in a pinch, and he opened one of the Alpo cans Shelby had left behind. He soaked the food in water and mashed it with his fork, and he used a chopstick from the Shanghai Gardens to bring the food to the bird's beak. It resisted at first. He had to work the stick against its mouth, and then it ate the meat. He'd forgotten how quick they were. It was like one of those sword swallowers at the circus how deep it took the stick.

She called him at four and again at four thirty and left messages on the machine. "I'm waiting," she said. "I've been here for hours." The second time she didn't say good-bye. She took a breath, and he heard the tears behind her voice. "You always do this, Jason. You always leave me hanging." He should have answered the phone.

She'd been planning this trip for weeks. There was still time to pick up the receiver, but he reached for the chopstick instead and fed the baby bird.

She hadn't taken her engagement ring. He'd worked three months to pay for that diamond, and she left it on the dresser. *Sell it,* she'd told him. *You need the money more than I do. The city doesn't pay you near enough for all the work you do.* He worked for the state and not the city. He worked for the Office of Weights and Measures. She could never keep that straight. He checked the scales and the packaged goods at every bakery from downtown to Fort Carson. He knew by feel if things were too light. His boss Milman called him Digit because his fingers were better than any scale.

He sent the ring to her certified mail, signature requested, and he kept the green slip when it came. He put it on the fridge next to the Dominos menu. She was growing organic vegetables and composting her coffee grounds, and he was eating deep-dish pizza and Dunkin' Donuts fritters. His pants were tight even when he left the top button open, and it didn't help that he was working the bakery rotation. His shirt smelled like cinnamon by the end of the day, and he was always hungry. He ate sticky buns in a single bite. He could unhinge his jaw like a snake. She'd give him a hard time when she saw him. Fat men have lower sperm counts, that's what she always said.

The bird started chirping at five in the morning. He fed it in the dark. Every twenty minutes he gave it a little more, and he could see the knot inside its throat where the food was gathered. The sky lightened through his window. There were streaks of pink above the maple trees, and it was the first sunrise he'd seen in years without feeling the need to hurry. Other birds were chirping outside, and the magpies were sharpening their beaks against his chimney. The vibrations worked their way down the metal flue. He drank his coffee in the kitchen. He sat at the empty table where she used to read her magazines. *We need to pay more attention to texture,* she'd say, and she looked so serious about the house. She talked about the Roman shades and the lacquer on the cupboards. The skateboard park bothered her when the city built it across the street. It would hurt their property values. She cared deeply about things he didn't even notice, but he didn't mind and he didn't complain because decorating kept her busy. If she focused on the house, maybe she wouldn't notice what was missing.

After the third time, she packed up the blankets and took apart the crib. The doctors said it was her hormone levels. They said her luteal phase was too short, but the creams and the pills didn't make it any longer. She started talking about caffeine and pesticides and hormones in dairy products. She ate only organic and stopped eating fish because of the mercury. *It's those environmental toxins,* she'd say. *They're disrupting all my cycles.*

Her friends were mothers, all of them. They named their kids Archer and Zephyr and Dax, and they talked only about mothering, as if they'd forgotten everything they'd ever cared about before. After a while Shelby stopped calling them, or maybe they stopped calling her, he wasn't really sure. She set her sticks aside and her basal thermometer, and she didn't mark the days down on her calendar. She was sleeping before he came to bed, and she was sleeping when he woke and he didn't reach for her. He'd forgotten how things were before they began trying. He'd forgotten how to touch her without thinking about her mucus first or whether she was spotting.

The walls of the nursery were still pale green, and she'd picked curtains from India that were stitched with butterflies and shells. Babies need light, she told him. They need to see the shadows moving on the walls. She knew about infants' brains and how they developed. She talked a lot about the importance of stimulation. It was a relief when she stopped reading her baby books. A relief and a sorrow both, and he didn't go inside that room. He left it the way it was.

He left her a message on her cell and told her he wasn't coming. "Something's come up," he said. "I'll call you when I can." But he didn't call her again or check his e-mail or go outside. He stayed in sweatpants and his hiking boots. He wore the clothes from his suitcase. It was better than going on a trip. He was camping inside his house, and nobody knew he was there. He didn't brush his teeth until noon. He didn't bother to shave. He explored the pantry shelves like a visitor, and he found things from before she'd gone organic. Ravioli in a can and niblets and Dinty Moore beef stew, an unopened package of Fig Newtons.

He watched the World's Strongest Man competition on cable. Just him and the bird sleeping in its nest. The men were pulling boxcars behind them and lifting the Atlas stones. They threw logs and kept the Hercules pillars from falling, and the guy from Iceland was winning again. The veins were bulging in his temples. Jason kept the bowl of mush beside him on the armrest. "How about you, Magnus," he said. "I bet it's time for more."

The bird opened its eyes. It knew his face already and the sound of the chopstick tapping against the bowl. It looked strange as a dinosaur with its pointed little head. Its beak was bright yellow, but its mouth was pale inside and Jason could see the blood pumping through its veins.

There was this girl who worked at the Gamburyan bakery on the way to the army base. Sometimes she went behind the store so she could feed the pigeons. They pecked around her feet, and she raised her arms when the bread was gone and swung her hips around. Jason had gone there for an inspection once, and he saw her dancing from his car. Her hair flew around her shoulders. It threw colors like oil on water. He gripped the wheel, and he didn't want to open the door or step outside. Her head was back and she was smiling and he wanted to know why. What brought her outside when it was cold and the wind had started to blow. She wasn't even wearing a jacket. What music was she hearing there in the alleyway?

Her name tag said Dalita. He saw it when he checked their scales. She wasn't older than twenty. They were cheating again on the cookies, but he didn't write them any tickets. He wrote things down in his notebook and checked the messages on his phone, but all he could see was this girl and how her hair was coming undone. She was a younger version of Shelby before Shelby became unhappy. He was distracted on his way out. He set his steel coffee mug on top of his car and left it there, and he drove that way across town. He grabbed Shelby when he got home. He tried to dance with her in the hall. *What's wrong with you,* she said. *Why are you acting so strange?* She smiled without meaning to, and he remembered the steps from the class they'd taken years before. Forward left and side right and they waltzed into the kitchen.

The days were full of sounds. Magpies on the chimney. Somebody practicing the drums every weekday at noon. Gardeners with their blowers because they were too lazy to use a rake. Delivery trucks backing up on the street and telephones ringing and hollow core doors slammed in the entryway. Contractors working a tile saw in the corner unit. He was living inside a hive and he hadn't ever noticed.

The fifth day the pin feathers really started sprouting. He brought the scale in and set the bird on the platform. He had a Tanita scale from when he used to work in silver. He still had his jewelers saw and his set of Nicholson files and sheets of copper and sterling in different gauges. Before she'd left he made her hammered silver cuffs and ash-trays they never used. Baby cups and feeding spoons that she gave away to her friends. The bird perched on the scale. It grabbed around the edge with one long witchy foot. It weighed less than ten grams. Not even a third of an ounce. It was lighter than powder when he lifted it up. Light as eight blueberries or a spoonful of sugar and he could feel the drumming of its heart.

His voicemail box was full. His father had called and both his older brothers, and Shelby was still trying. He cleared out the messages one by one. He didn't check his mailbox in the lobby or log on to his e-mail account. He didn't have a single place to be. This was how life used to be when he was only eight. The summers were so long, and he didn't have camp yet like his two older brothers. No art classes or trombone lessons, just a string of dusty afternoons in his spot beneath the trees. His mother was working in the dress shop and his dad was still in the army and he was alone in the house most days. He spent hours on the backyard lounger. He read Asimov and *Weird Tales*, and there was nothing better. Frozen pizzas and pudding pops and those storms rolling down from Palmer Lake. The air shimmered sometimes. It was sweet like butterscotch from the ponderosa pines. His mother would call him from work before the thunder started. She'd tell him not to be afraid. She didn't need to watch the weather to know when one was coming because she could feel them in her bunion. Ten years had passed and his father still talked about her in the present tense.

The bird was getting bigger. It was hopping on his floor. Its feathers were in, and it ate from a bowl and not just from his hand. He set it on the window sill so it could see what it was missing. "Look what's out there," he said. "Everything's blooming, but it's not too hot. This is the best time of the year." He rubbed his chin, and pretty soon his beard would be full like Jeremiah Johnson's. It was really coming in. Who knew there'd be so much gray.

Last summer a pregnant woman in Omaha lost her balance and fell from her bedroom loft. Her husband was a musician. She landed on a microphone stand down in the living room. The metal passed through her abdomen and came out between her shoulders. She survived and her son did, too. He was born healthy and unmarked. Another inch either way and it would have speared her baby or her liver or her heart. There was a lesson to be learned from this story. He watched the news so he could understand. Sometimes things are fragile and sometimes they're resilient and who knew why this bird had lived when all the others had died. His father smoked two packs a day and he'd been exposed to Agent Orange, but it was his mother whose lungs had failed. Women did drugs and fell down stairs and birthed their healthy babies, and at their core things were a mystery. He needed to rise above them. He needed distance to see their pattern.

The bird learned to fly when he wasn't watching. It was the last Saturday of his vacation. He came in from the bathroom, and it was sitting on top of the TV cabinet. It looked at him with those rust-colored eyes.

It flew from the cabinet to the sofa and back again. It flew as if it had been flying for a thousand years, as if gravity were a riddle and it knew the answer from birth. "Look at you," Jason said. He stretched out his arm like a falconer, but the bird didn't come to his wrist.

They started calling from work on Monday at 9:30 in the morning. His boss Milman wanted to know where he was. *Personnel had you down for ten days,* the secretary said. She coughed a little and cleared her throat. *Maybe they have it wrong.* By noon Milman himself was calling. *It's not like you,* he was saying. Eleven and a half years at Weights and Measures and Jason had never taken a sick day. Not even when he had mono or when Shelby lost the babies. He should have stayed with her those first few days. Nobody needed to tell him this. They should have talked more or gone together on a trip, but he'd gone to work instead and wrote up his bakery tickets.

Milman called all Monday afternoon and then again on Tuesday. When the ringing became too much and the flashing of the light, Jason unplugged his cordless phone and set it in the closet. He wedged it between the beach towels, and the house went quiet then. Even the bird stopped its singing.

Any time now they'd contact his next of kin. They'd reach Shelby or his father and ask whether he was okay. They might ask the police to send a cruiser by. He could explain things away, but he lacked the will. He could blame it on a fever or a case of stomach flu, and he'd be back on his rounds. Maybe he'd see Dalita bringing the birds down from their wires. The Mesa Mercado would still be charging a dime too much for golden raisins. They had a problem with their scanner. And the bakery at the downtown Farmers Market mislabeled the sourdough loaves. A nickel here and a quarter there and there weren't enough inspectors to keep the stores honest. He could spend all his days going from one place to the next, and it wasn't any use because people were the problem and not just the machines.

He opened the door and stepped out onto the balcony. It was Wednesday morning just before seven and the air was already warm.

Another perfect summer day. One of thousands in his life. He was forty-one years old, and he'd have another thirty summers maybe, another forty if he was lucky. The bird jumped from the counter to the floor. It followed him outside and hopped onto the glass table. If two had lived and not just one, they'd fly away together, but a single bird wouldn't leave. It knew no face but his. He wanted to tell Shelby that he missed her. Not the way she was now but the way she used to be. He wanted to tell her to be grateful.

In another hour all the noises would start again. The contractors would come in their white trucks and the gardeners with their blowers. But right now there was nobody in the courtyard or walking on the street. Just a kid at the skate park who had the place to himself. A skinny kid with plaid shorts so loose they'd fall down if he wasn't careful. He moved like a pendulum when he turned on the concrete. He moved like an ocean wave. Physics could explain his movements. It could map out the forces and the curves, but it didn't reach things at their core. What could science say about something like grace.

Mourning the Departed

Filipina ladies made the best funeral dishes. Sausages and beef with bananas and garlicky noodles, and once he went to a funeral where they cooked a pig up whole and people stood around and fought for the cracklings. The German widows did a nice job, too, with all their butter cakes. His choice today was limited, though. Mexican and Korean, and he wasn't going to eat that spicy Korean food again. He'd gone once to a funeral at their Baptist church up on Academy, and all they had was fishy balls and little silver fish that still had their heads. He was sick afterward for days, and he'd go to his own funeral before another Korean one, that much was certain.

He stood by the buffet and plucked tamales from the pot with a dented pair of tongs. It was a teenager named Marco who had died. The driver was drunk probably when he hit the boy. It happened at three in the afternoon right by the Citadel Mall, and the driver kept on going and didn't stop and the police were searching for his truck.

The young ones were the hardest. They were students, some of them, or newlyweds. They left babies behind and pretty wives who swayed beside the coffin. It was easier with the vets from his Korean War group. They were dropping every other week now, and people were sorry but they weren't surprised. He looked around the room, at the high schoolers in their dress shirts and the parents who couldn't be forty yet judging from their faces. All those funerals he'd gone to, for kids and old soldiers and mothers who died too young, and those grieving relatives who filled their plates but didn't eat. He took it all in. He swallowed their sorrows whole, and sometimes he tried to cry but the tears didn't come.

He found a chair in the back of the hall. They'd set up card tables near the front, and that's where the family sat and the mother was weeping again and the other ladies gathered around her to rub her shoulders and stroke her wavy hair. They weren't at the funeral hall this time and there'd be no graveside ceremony either, not with the snow still coming down and the ground harder than marble. They'd need jackhammers to break through. He balanced a paper plate across his knee, and another lady sat down beside him and fumbled in her purse. She pulled out a wrinkled Kleenex. She looked at him while she blew her nose. Loud as a trumpet the way she sounded. She eyed him like a bill collector, and for a moment he wanted to stand and leave.

"It's a shame," he said. He shifted in his chair. "Not even eighteen and he's gone."

"I was his teacher," she said. "Three years I taught him piano." She set her purse down.

He watched her fingers. They were long as a surgeon's, but the knuckles were already beginning to show and they'd be knobby before she was old. They'd be crooked like his mother's had been. That's why she'd worn gloves every day, even in summertime. Thin white cotton ones with lace around the top, and he hadn't gone to her funeral, but his sister told him that's how she was buried, too. In her prettiest summer pair. "It's a shame," he said again.

"I taught him on the day he died." She pulled another tissue from her pack. "I was running late. Three years and I was always on time and that Tuesday I was late."

"Let's hope they find the driver." He poked around the tamale and found a stringy piece of pork.

"If I'd been on time that day, he'd be here still. He'd be home with his mother."

"That's not how things work," he said. "If his time was up then it was up for sure, and it didn't matter when your lesson ended." The car would have found its way to him, he wanted to say. If not that one then another one and the ending would have been the same.

She looked at him, but kindly this time, and her eyes were pale as his Evelyn's. "You look familiar. Are you a teacher from the school?"

"I'm retired," he said. "On Thursdays I volunteer at the DAV."

"I have a memory for faces."

"You might have seen me at Safeway," he said. "Every Wednesday I go for the coupons." It was time to move to another chair. Time to leave and soak his feet because they were beginning to burn again. Another half hour and he'd be limping to his car, but he stayed where he was because he wanted to hear her voice some more. She was a music teacher, and he wanted her to sing.

She pointed over his shoulder at the streamers and balloons that hung from the ceiling tiles. "It's strange having balloons at a funeral."

"Maybe that's how they do it down in Mexico. Maybe they like it festive," he said. "I went to this funeral once where they had sparklers and firecrackers and a bar with champagne."

He stopped then, and his cheeks went hot. It wasn't right to talk about his hobby, how he went to funerals instead of visiting Evelyn, who lay alone in a private room. Just last year she'd stopped recognizing him and she loved another man in the unit anyway, a retired policeman who still had all his hair and he was as forgetful as she was, God help him. They were perfect together how they sat in their wheelchairs and held hands over the lunch table. Her pale eyes were clear again, and she laughed at all the old policeman's jokes. It was easier going to funerals than visiting her, than reading paperback books or calling his sons, who didn't want to hear from him and they were never home anyway. He went to funerals and comforted the mourners and ate their food, and when he came home the tightness was gone from his chest. He was contented again, and he sat in his kitchen and soaked his feet in Epsom salts to keep the sting away.

"I'm sorry. It sounds like you've lost a lot of friends."

Even his ears were burning now. "I'll be eighty next March." He looked at the window, and the wind was blowing flakes sideways against the glass. It was cold as Korea outside but not as damp. All those nights along the reservoir and the sky was bright with flares, all light and no warmth, and almost sixty years later his legs were still wrecked from the cold and from the shoe pacs that had frozen and torn away his skin. "We're dropping like leaves."

"I suppose that's true," she said. "But look at Marco. There are no guarantees not even for the young."

He looked at her hands again, at her ring finger. She wasn't wearing any band, and his eyes moved up to her face and that's when he saw the two hammered bands on a chain around her neck. He straightened up in his chair. He drew his shoulders back. "Are you married?" He asked the question without meaning to. He was watching those two yellow rings, and he needed to know.

"My husband died. It's been four years." She reached for the bands and clasped her hand around them.

She'd changed her hair since the funeral, he could see it now. She'd let it go to gray and her face was thinner and not as round, but even from the back of the funeral home he'd seen those eyes and he remembered them still. He felt a little queasy. His stomach rumbled, and he regretted eating the pork and especially those refried beans. "I'm sorry," he said.

She tilted her head again. "What about you? I bet you're a grandpa."

He nodded. "Two sons and four grandsons I never see. They're out in Wisconsin and too busy to visit."

"Well maybe *you* should visit them." She was smiling a little now. "If those folks at the DAV will cut you loose for a Thursday or two." She got up and straightened out her skirt, brushing it with her palms. She went to the mother and crouched beside her chair. She stayed there for a long while and the mother began to rock again, but without sobbing this time or making any sound. The teacher stood back up. She set her hand on her hip and stared at him.

He needed to stop with the obituaries. Start up his trains again or the radio Evelyn had bought him years before. His antenna was still up though old Schneider next door fussed about how it took away his mountain view. *I don't want to see wires and metal,* he'd say, *I just want to see my Pikes Peak.* They stopped talking after that and he let the weeds grow in the back alley just to spite Schneider and his wife, the chickweed in the spring and the carpetweed and curly dock in the summertime, and all the sprays and fertilizer they used couldn't stop the spread.

She came back to him, carrying two cups of punch. "Just look how it's coming down," she said. "No wonder people get sad this time of year. They need those special lamps to remind them there's a sun."

"Nothing wrong with the cold." He took a cup from her. "So long as you've got the right clothes for it." His feet were starting to tingle now. He couldn't feel his toes.

"I went to India once," she said. "Everything was brighter there. The sky and the clothes and even the food. Three weeks and I didn't see any gray."

"I've been to Korea. That was enough for me."

"My husband liked to travel. Every year we took a trip."

He nodded. He remembered all the slides she'd had at the service, from India and Egypt, too, and even Vietnam. They were drinking from coconuts and swimming on beaches where soldiers had died forty years before, and the water looked beautiful, he had to agree. It was blue as Evelyn's eyes.

"Even the funerals are bright there. The ladies wear colors and not black." She drank from her cup. "And there are these mourners the family sometimes hires. Strangers who come to pay their last respects." She smiled at him, and he was certain that she knew.

"I'd better be going," he said. "I'm hobbling already." He was distracted when he said good-bye, and he took the wrong way home. He took Academy which he never did because he didn't like the traffic and the lights weren't synchronized right. He was home already before he realized he'd never learned her name.

He filled his soaking tub right away. He poured the salts in and sat on his chair, and after a while the numbness turned to burning just like it did the first time he froze his feet. He looked at the phone and the curtains Evelyn had sewn years before for the narrow window above the kitchen sink. *It's no work doing the dishes when I can see the mountains,* she always said. *Those millionaires in Kissing Camels don't have a better view.* His sons were probably home already and watching their evening shows, and Evelyn was laughing with her policeman in the nursing home, and somewhere in the city the music teacher was thinking of India where it didn't snow and the sky was never gray.

Slowly, slowly the feeling came back to his feet. The burning became a tingling, and he could move them now in the water. He reached for his towel. He reached across the table and saw his reflection in the dark window glass, and he cried.

Sidewinder

He walked the field beside his house with a shovel and a bucket. Today he was looking for Apache tears. The dirt was fine as powder, but it gave him trouble when he tried to dig. A little ways down and it was solid. It resisted even when he stepped on the shovel or when he used his pick. Sometimes he found mica or pieces of quartz, and he dropped them in his backpack. He'd look them up later in his book. Mr. Redding next door had given him a book about crystals and a small prospector's pick. *Don't tell your stepdad where you got these,* he said. *I don't want him getting mad.* Mr. Redding knew rocks. He used to hunt for zircons up on the Gold Camp Road. He'd worked the mines before he enlisted, but now he was retired. He sat on his patio most days and drank coffee from an old green thermos.

It was July, and all those days without school blended one into the next. His mother wanted to sign him up for swimming lessons, or maybe drawing at the community center. *He needs some structure,* she said. *Next month he'll be eleven and he needs some other kids around,* but he was relieved when she stopped talking about summer school or going over to the pool. Life was easier in the house when she let things go. And he wanted only his bucket anyway. A chance to work the dirt. There were Indians here once. They hunted buffalo and fought their battles, and maybe they left some arrowheads behind. You could buy them for three dollars at the rock store out by Ute Pass, but this summer he wanted to find his own.

He had a juice box today and a cold cream soda, but he didn't stop to drink. In another few hours the clouds would come in, and she'd call him inside because of the thunder. It was dangerous in the field with all those power lines. A boy in Pueblo had gotten hit just standing under a tree. *Don't make me worry,* she'd say. *I've got enough on my mind,* and she'd kiss his forehead and push the bangs out from his eyes. He stepped on the shovel with all his weight and gathered up the dirt, working through it with his fingers the way prospectors did. It was clumps mostly and bits of broken glass. Some of the glass was worn smooth like pebbles, and he kept the nicest pieces, the ones that were green or wavy with air bubbles.

He was almost done with his first pile. He was ready to make a new hole when he lifted up something smooth. He wiped away the dust, and it was no bigger than his thumbnail and shaped just like a tear. He held it up to the light. It looked like honey in the sun. He examined it for spiders inside or signs of ancient insects. He'd learned about amber in school. How it was magnetic if you rubbed it and how it had caught things as it dried. But this piece here wasn't amber and it had nothing sealed inside. It was clear until he moved it, and then it flashed orange and brown.

The stone heated up as he worked. It felt like those hand warmers she gave him when he shoveled the neighbors' walks. He moved it from pocket to pocket, and it didn't cool, not even when he rested in the shade and drank his soda pop. All those days digging holes and sifting through the piles, and he finally had his Apache tear. It was prettier than the pictures in his book. It was gold and not just black, and sometimes it went milky before clearing up again. He took it with him when the storm clouds came and she called him from the door.

There were rules about how the table was set and when the shades were pulled. Dinner had to be ready at seven exactly, and if he talked before the meat was cut his mother had to shush him. *Be quiet, Jesse,* she'd say. *Wait until we've eaten.* His stepdad Russell didn't like it when he talked at meals. He heard talk all day at the Toyota dealership, and at home he wanted quiet. He didn't like it if the TV remote was on the coffee table instead of in the wicker basket or if the car was parked too close to his truck. Sometimes she parked it crooked, and he made her do it again.

She made spaghetti with meatballs, turkey because Russell didn't eat beef. Red meat could stay inside you for years, he said. It really clogged you up. Pepper flakes were bad, too, because they made his eczema flare. Jesse was careful with his noodles. He didn't want to spill any sauce. He watched his mother to make sure things were okay. He looked to see if her arms were covered. Russell didn't like short sleeves not even in the summer. After dinner Russell would sit in front of the TV and maybe she'd have a little time. They could sit together in his room, and he'd show her the rock he'd found and how it was warm still from the sun.

His mom and Russell fought once he was back inside his room. It always began with something small. Maybe she left the dish brush on the countertop. Maybe she forgot to open all the mail. Russell was talking in his quiet voice. He never shouted, not even when he threw things against the wall. His mother talked and Russell was talking, too, and the conversation moved from room to room. Jesse sat on his bean bag chair and tried hard not to listen. He cupped the stone inside his palm, and it was getting warmer. She was standing in the hallway just outside his door. She went to the living room and Russell went, too, and that's where she began to shout. Jesse held the stone tighter. She shouldn't shout. She needed to be quiet, and he closed his eyes so she could hear his warning. "I don't know what you want from me," she was saying. "I'm doing everything I can."

He knew what would happen next. The air had that black electrical feel. Jesse listened to the TV instead of his mother's voice. He tried to make out the words. Mattresses were on sale, and now was the time to buy back-to-school clothes at JCPenney. The commercials sounded muffled through the walls of his room. They sounded like another language. He held that stone, and his mother was crying and it was hot inside his hand.

Mr. Redding grew snap peas every summer and pots with fat red and yellow tomatoes. He had hummingbird feeders on all his windows and seed tubes for the finches. His belly was enormous even with all the work he did in his yard. It looked hard like a basketball or a summer melon. *Lean Cuisines for dinner,* he'd say, *and look how fat I am.* He kept a jug with black tea brewing on the table. It sat there in the sun next to his coffee thermos, and when people came to visit he brought out ice cubes and sugar. Sometimes when Jesse came by he set out Nutter Butters, too, and cookies from a tin. Nothing homemade because Mrs. Redding had died without writing down her recipes.

Jesse was sunburnt from working the field. He picked at his nose which had started to peel. They sat together on the patio once the sun had gone below the trees. It was cool in Mr. Redding's yard. The grape vines twisted on their wires, and they were sour as pickles those grapes. All skin and seeds, but Mr. Redding cut the clusters when they were ripe. He ate them with sugar and Jesse did, too, and they spit the seeds into a plastic cup. Jesse moved his chair closer to the table. The pavers had started to settle, and the patio was a little crooked. Jesse showed him the stone. He took it out of his pocket and laid it next to the pitcher. "I found an Apache tear," he said. "Look how clear it is."

Mr. Redding lifted it up and held it close to his face. He squinted like somebody aiming a gun. "That's no Apache tear." He turned it around in his fingers and felt it with his thumb. "It looks like a fire agate maybe or one of them yellow opals."

Mr. Redding got up from his chair. His pants hung low around his belly, but he didn't pull them up. He brought out his rock book. He whistled a little through his teeth, and Jesse stood beside him and looked at the pages, too.

"It's a mystery," Mr. Redding said. "You need somebody smarter than me to help you figure this one out." It couldn't be opals, he was saying. You have to go farther west for those. Up to Idaho where the lava used to flow or down to Mexico, and it couldn't be fire agate either because they grow deep inside the bedrock. That's some hard rock mining there. It takes heavy equipment to dig them up.

Jesse took the stone back. He knew what it was even if Mr. Redding didn't. It was a teardrop. An Apache lady cried when she lost her boy in battle. She cried and left a crystal, and now it belonged to him.

"Tell me about the snakes again," Jesse said. He reached for a sour grape. "About that time you went on maneuver."

"Maybe later." Mr. Redding finished his tea and set his glass next to Jesse's, which was empty, too. "Maybe another time when you come." He didn't refill the glasses, and Jesse knew it was time.

Mr. Redding waved, but he didn't get up. He rocked in his redwood chair. "Come see me if you need me," he said. "It don't matter if it's late."

His mother had started taking classes at H&R Block. She went on Wednesday afternoons, and she said it was their secret. They'd go for ice cream once she had her certification. She'd be done in September and they'd go on the West Side to the creamery and eat at the sundae buffet, but he needed to keep quiet in the meantime. He had to take care of himself those four hours every week. She was at Safeway if anybody asked. Safeway and the pharmacy and she'd be home any minute. She said it, and she grabbed his hand, but he already knew. It was a secret like his teardrop, and they'd go driving when she was done. They'd leave Colorado and go to Arizona and maybe farther west. She'd have marketable skills. That's what she called it. She'd find a job from nine to five and help folks with their taxes.

They'd make stops along the way. She'd show him the Four Corners where the Indians had built houses in the cliffs. They'd go sledding in the sand dunes. And there was a forest of petrified trees and petrified forest rangers guarded them, and she laughed when she said it. She laughed, and her eyes were like amber. They were flecked with orange and brown, and she held his wrist so tight it started hurting, but he didn't pull away.

It was the hottest August on record. That's what the newscasters said. People stayed inside and slept down in their basements, but Jesse didn't mind. He carried the stone when he rode his bike and when he worked in the field. It was like one of those crystal balls the fortunetellers use. He looked into it, and the colors were always different. He saw his mom and she was taking notes in class and he saw her when she cried. She'd parked someplace he didn't know, and she was slumped behind the wheel. The rock was older than his mom and Mr. Redding or anybody else alive in the world. Old as the pyramids or those big redwoods on the coast.

The snakes they like the gentle light. At night they come out from their holes. Mr. Redding rocked in his chair. His hands were folded across his belly, and he was sweating even in the shade. It was an August day like this one, maybe even hotter. A hundred twenty men somewhere east of Pueblo. He was just an E-3 back then and skinny as a noodle. They slipped sometimes because their boots had leather soles. Nothing like those sneaker boots the army uses now. They slipped with all their gear and it was stranger than Mars how the rocks were shaped and the dirt was red and gray. There were coral snakes and rattlers out there. He could see their tracks where the sand was soft.

Jesse reached into the grape bowl. He used Mr. Redding's Swiss Army knife to cut himself a cluster. Mr. Redding was in a chatting mood. He was telling all his stories.

It was just before sunset, and he'd gone behind the tents so he could take a pee. That's when he saw it coiled beside his boot. So close he could see the horns above its eyes and how it moved its rattle. He stood there with his pants open, and the snake reared back its head. "I never saw a thing like that," Mr. Redding said. "How it moved like a single muscle." He shook his head like the snake was a beautiful thing. He'd be dead as Abe Lincoln if it got him. He'd die alone behind those army tents. But something happened in that moment. Something kept the snake from biting or coming any closer. It moved away instead. It unspooled itself and slid across the sand. It went away like water, Mr. Redding said. Like one of them belly dancers.

It was two days before he could piss again. His insides were clenched up tight. And still he was grateful afterward. Even the army rations tasted good. "Look how strange the world is," Mr. Redding said. "You don't know when God's grace will touch you. It can raise us if we let it." And Jesse nodded, but he didn't agree. It wasn't grace that saved Mr. Redding. No, the snake was just being a snake, and maybe it found something better.

Mr. Redding looked tired when Jesse left. He slumped a little in his chair. He pointed to the Swiss Army knife on the redwood table.

"That one there has got your name on it," he said. "The day you turn twelve it's yours."

Don't look at Russell or his fat white hands. Don't look at the marks on his cheeks. *Those aren't pimples,* he always said. *It's the caffeine that makes me flare.* Build a fort and hide inside. Use your desk chair and your table. Use milk crates if you have them and extra blankets from the closet. You'll come out when he's gone. When you hear the truck door close and the music from his radio. On Wednesdays when she's at class you'll stay outside even if it storms. Droplets big as quarters and they'll puddle up your field. The wind will blow, and you'll dig through that mud and work it with your fingers.

The tomatoes in Mr. Redding's front yard were parched. Their leaves had started to curl, and Jesse took the watering can and emptied it into their pots. Mr. Redding wasn't out back. He hadn't been out there all day. Flies were gathering around the old man's tea. They were pulled in by the sugar, and one was floating inside the glass.

Jesse knocked on the patio door. "Mr. Redding," he said. "I found a piece of mica." He slid the door partway open. "You won't believe it when you see."

The house was dark the way Mr. Redding liked it. The window units were all running. It was cool inside, and when Jesse stepped into the kitchen he saw the old man's foot. It was sticking out from the bedroom doorway. It was blue and swollen like a water balloon, with the skin stretched tight across his ankle. Jesse came a little closer. The old man had fallen just inside his bedroom. He lay on his back like somebody taking a nap. His eyes were open and covered with strange brown spots, and all around him were Tylenol pills from the bottle in his hand.

His mom said sometimes our brains get hurt. Sometimes we bleed too much up there, and other times our blood gets clotted and can't make its way through. That's what happened to Mr. Redding. His brain got starved of blood, and now he's gone to a better place. He's gone to be with Mrs. Redding and they're back together the way they used to be. She stroked Jesse's hair when she talked. "Sometimes people go away," she said. "They leave the earth and go to heaven, and you keep them in your heart." Jesse stopped listening when she started talking about heaven. He went inside his room.

Mr. Redding's three nieces came from Durango and started packing up his house. They had the U-Hauls parked, and their husbands moved the boxes. They didn't water the tomato plants or pick the last grape clusters. Jesse went over there when they left for the day. He watered the lawn with the hose. Mr. Redding wouldn't be happy with the way things were going. His lawn was already brown. Jesse watered the garden the way Mr. Redding would want, and he weeded between the grapevines. The birds still came even after the feeders were empty. The blue jays and the finches and all the roses dropped their petals, and his mother was wrong, he knew it for certain. All her talk about heaven like it was someplace far away. Heaven was here on this crooked patio where Mr. Redding used to sit.

Three rose quartz crystals and a milky chunk of chalcedony. Mica that splintered if he wasn't careful. A piece of agate with black squiggles that looked like a ponderosa pine. A bucket of green and amber glass that was smooth around the edges, but no arrowhead, not a single one, and no other Apache tears. He sorted the crystals and kept them in egg cartons on his desk, and each new thing he found was a reminder that summer was almost over. After Labor Day he'd be back in school.

There wasn't any reason why Russell came home early that last Wednesday before the holiday weekend. His truck came up the street, and it wasn't even half past four. Jesse was digging. He was filling up his buckets. The driveway was empty because his mother was still at class, and Russell came out with his lunchbox and his big metal thermos. He pounded on the door. Jesse set his shovel down. He crouched between the holes. The street was empty except for two of Mr. Redding's nieces, who were sitting in the shade. They fanned themselves with magazines and drank tea from the old man's pitcher. Russell pounded with one hand and fished in his pocket with the other, and his face was splotchy from the coffee he drank. Jesse could see the marks all the way across the field.

He came running before Russell called. "Where is she?" Russell was asking, and his cheeks were redder than they'd ever been before. Jesse opened the door for him, and Russell went straight into the kitchen. He leaned against the sink and pushed the curtains back.

"She's at Target," Jesse said.

Russell turned around. "Why didn't you go with?"

"I dunno." Jesse stood there, and he held out both his hands. "I didn't feel like it today. My throat's a little sore."

"Call her." Russell pointed to the phone. Water was dripping from the faucet, and it was the only sound inside the house.

"I think she went to Safeway, too," Jesse said. All his mother's warnings and he didn't remember what he was supposed to say. "She went to Safeway and the pharmacy to see about my throat."

Russell took the phone from the cradle. He set the phone to speaker and gave it to Jesse, who dialed her cell phone number.

"Sweetie," his mother said. She was talking in a low voice, just a little louder than a whisper. "Is everything okay? You're not supposed to call when I'm in class. My teacher doesn't like it."

"Things are fine," Russell told her. "They couldn't be any better."

You need to know the difference between bad snakes and the good ones. Sometimes they look alike. You have to watch for the little things. You need to pay attention. The bad ones have flat heads usually, and their skin is different colors, except for water snakes but they don't matter because they don't live up in the mountains. Mr. Redding always said Colorado was better than Florida and those other states down South. Snake pits, he called them, but the barbecue was good. Mr. Redding knew the snake rhymes, and he taught Jesse how they went. *Red touches yellow it can kill a fellow, but red touches black is okay for Jack.* The old man's voice was lousy from the cigarettes he used to smoke, but he sang anyway and Jesse sang along. They ate sour grapes together and rocked in the redwood chairs, and the air was soft the way it sometimes gets. Jesse was sorry when the sun went down and when his mother called. *Come see me tomorrow*, the old man said. *Come show me what you find.*

The last time he heard her voice she was working in the kitchen. "What's wrong with my taking a class," she was asking, but it didn't sound like a question. "I was only trying to help." She talked about how sales were slow at the dealership, and she'd make $7.50 an hour doing taxes plus a ten percent commission on every return. That was good money. Better than she could hope for, and she'd wait until Jesse was back in school and she wouldn't neglect the house. The faucet started and stopped again. She started the dishwasher and closed the cabinet doors too hard. Jesse heard it all from his room.

"Maybe I should leave," she was saying. "I should have done it years ago," and Jesse wanted her to stop. He set his hands together the way the nuns had taught him at the Divine Redeemer school. He was only six then. It was a long long time ago, before his daddy left and his mother met Russell and they moved into this house. He prayed, and there was a crashing in the hallway and the sound of breaking dishes. There were thumps against the wall like somebody was knocking.

She'd come for him any second now. They'd walk together out the door and drive into the desert. They'd take the highways where the prospectors went a hundred years before. Where the Indians fought their battles and left behind their tears. She'd talked about how the dunes looked just as the sun goes down. *The sand is soft as powder*, she said. *It changes with the wind.* Her eyes were gold and she reached for him, and sometimes she held his wrist so tight her fingertips left bruises.

There wasn't any lock on Jesse's door. He set a chair beneath the knob how they did it in the movies. He tilted it until the fit was tight, and then he turned off all his lights. He went inside his fort where it was darker still. He sat in there and waited, and he could hear the beating of his heart. He waited some more, and a golden light was shining through the blanket walls. He poked his head out and looked. It came from the doorway and the window. It came from the stone that was sitting on his desk. It moved like firelight against the walls. It flickered and cast strange shadows.

There were footsteps in the hallway and the sound of something heavy being pulled across the floor. The screen door opened with a bang. It opened and closed, and more footsteps came and they stopped right outside his room. The light was getting brighter. Jesse stood up and went to the door. He wanted to cover his eyes. The knob began to turn. Russell was standing on the other side. Jesse could see the shadows from his boots in the crack beneath the door.

Jesse reached for the knob. He felt it turn inside his hand. He squeezed it harder, with all the strength he had, and Russell was breathing on the other side of the door. The planks creaked under his boots. They stood like that, the two of them, and Jesse didn't let go. He held the knob even after it had stopped turning. After the shadows were gone from under the door and Russell had started up his truck. The room went dark and the stone did, too. The dishwasher finished its cycle.

Jesse was still holding the doorknob when the policemen came. It was warm outside, but they covered his shoulders with a blanket. Two cruisers with their lights flashing and they took him to the station. They let him take the stone along, and it was cold inside his hand. A lady doctor came and asked him questions. She wanted to know about school and his mom and his favorite TV shows. She bent down beside his chair. "I hear you know about crystals," she said. "They tell me you're an expert," but he didn't open his hand for her. He didn't let her see it.

Lay My Head

Babies weren't frightened of her face. They didn't yet know sickness. They saw only her eyes, how big they were. There was a baby girl before her in the aisle. A little round-faced girl, no older than two. Her ponytail went straight up like a paint brush, and her mother had tied a pink ribbon around it. The girl stood up on the seat while her mother read magazines. Angela smiled at her. She set aside her book and covered her eyes with her fingers and uncovered them again. The little girl giggled at that. She grabbed the fabric of the headrest and squealed. She reached for Angela and for the stewardess who was pushing the drinks cart up the aisle. Her mother patted her on the bottom. *Felicia Marie,* she said. *You better hush. People are trying to sleep.* The girl squealed again, and her cheeks were dimpled and shiny like apples. The mother looked between the seats then. Her face went dark when she saw Angela. *Get down here, young lady,* the mother said. *Get down here right now,* and she moved quickly. She pulled her little girl away from the headrest. She held her baby against her chest. She held her there and didn't let her squirm.

The roundness in Angela's cheeks went first. Her skin went from olive to yellow. She'd spent all those mornings on her deck, but the sun didn't warm her, not even in September when LA was hottest. She'd shivered and watched the neighbor kids splash around in the pool.

They worked their squirt guns and wrestled in the water, and they were happy even when their parents fought. How little children need to be happy. How little it takes, and still things go wrong. She watched them all summer and into fall, and the roundness was gone and from one day to the next the veins popped out on her forearms. Her hands were spotted like her grandma's had been. Liver spots, grandma called them, and Angela had wondered why.

Her belly grew round like a pregnant lady's. Like Mr. Hogan from the old neighborhood who drank beer every morning and tossed the cans onto his wife's compost heap. In the last few weeks the bones in her throat had started to show. There was a hollow between them, and her mother would notice this right away. She'd see it and know. Thirty years married to a U.S. soldier, and her mother still thought like a German farm girl. She'd been right about Angela's father. She knew he was sick from the smell of his breath. *He's got the mark*, she'd said. She knew it months before the doctors did, and she'd see the mark on Angela now, too. Her girl who'd been pretty once. She should be a model, that's what all the people said. And what did it matter. Every day brought another loss, and her prettiness was the least of them. It fell away like the burden it was.

Her mother was waiting at the luggage carousel. She carried the same winter coat, the extra one she kept for guests because it was cold even in November. Angela didn't remember that old plaid coat until she saw her mother standing there in her winter boots. She'd brought it along every Christmas when Angela came home from college. *Look how you're dressed*, she'd say back then. *You're always in short sleeves. You need to cover up.* Angela would pretend she didn't feel the wind when they went through the sliding glass doors. She'd say she was warm in her sandals or the loafers she wore without socks. Anything was better than letting her mother be right.

The coat smelled like mothballs. It was years between visits now. Years when it used to be months. Her mother walked too quickly at first. Angela couldn't keep up, and the air outside was sharp in her throat. It squeezed her chest. She'd forgotten how thin the air could be up here. This was probably how fish felt when they were pulled from the water. She slowed and stopped and set her hand against the retaining wall where the juniper bushes grew. Her mother stopped, too. She came close and fixed the collar on the old plaid coat. She took her scarf off and wrapped it around Angela's neck, and her eyes were black when she spoke. "You need to cover your mouth," she said. "The wind's picking up. All those years in California and you've forgotten how it blows." They walked slowly to the car. Her mother always parked in one of the farthest spots, out by the long-term lot. There were patches of ice in places. Angela slipped and caught herself, and the mountains were dark already against the sky.

Her bed was the same and the feather quilt, but her books were gone and most of her posters and ribbons. Her mother had packed these things in plastic boxes and set them in the closet. The bookshelves were full with her mother's art books now and porcelain figurines, and up at the top there was the yellow book of fairy tales her mother had brought from Germany. She'd read it to Angela when she was little. She read to her in German, and Angela understood. Struwwelpeter with his wild hair and Hans im Glück who was happiest when all his gold was lost. She knew the stories and her mother's voice, and that was the last thing she heard that night and the first thing in the morning.

Her body was healthy in every way but one. She wasn't even forty and her heart was healthy and her lungs were clear and everything was perfect except for the thing that wasn't.

She held a cup of tea in her lap. Whitethorn and lemon balm because they were good for the circulation, that's what her mother told her. Her mother had set the redwood chaise in the middle of the yard. She'd brought out blankets, too, and wrapped them around Angela's knees. It was almost forty degrees out, and it felt even warmer. The sun was shining on her head. It was bright as California outside, mountain bright, and she should have worn her sunglasses. Two little girls played in the front yard at the old Meyer house. They tunneled into the melting snow. One of them was wearing a skirt without any tights, and even from across the street Angela could see the pink of her legs. The Meyers had moved years before and who knew what happened to Patty, fat Patty who was round as a bowling ball but completely flat-chested. They called her Fatricia at school. Angela did, too. Only once but it was wrong and she knew it even then. She did things when she was young as if she had no choice. A couple of the girls painted Patty's face one day in gym class. *Close your eyes,* they'd told her. *Stand real still,* and Patty waited for them to make her pretty. Calm as a Buddha while she stood there by the mirror. She waited for them to melt the eyeliner. They used Bic lighters back then to get the flow just right, and Angela didn't want to look. She put her jeans back on, those extra-slim Jordache jeans that cut high across her waist. She combed her hair and waited by the lockers for the bell to ring. They were working on Patty's eyes. They nudged each other and laughed at the enormous arches they drew and the red circles they put across her cheeks, and Angela saw it all and she didn't stop them and she didn't say a thing, not even to Patty who stood there with a crooked dreamy smile. She left before Patty opened her eyes. She went out of the locker room and into the courtyard where the smokers waited between classes.

The little girls were running circles now. They shouted and poked their fingers through the links of the fence. Their mother was looking out the living room window. She held a baby against her shoulder. Angela waved to be neighborly. She raised her hand and the woman waved back without knowing who Angela was and then she called her girls inside. It was dinnertime. *It's getting colder,* she told them. *Quit your running and come.* She hustled them in and shut the door.

Angela leaned back against the chair. The lights went on in all the houses and she should be getting inside, but she stayed because the evening air smelled like winter. Like pine needles and chimney smoke. Somewhere a dog barked and another answered, and she held her cup and looked at the old Meyer house which hadn't been painted in years. The screens hung away from the windows in places. The house looked tired and the street, too, and the sky was pink above them with fading traces of the sun.

•

Her mother talked about transplants in the evenings. This was their routine. They sat together in the kitchen, and her mother said Angela needed to get on the list. *It's time,* she said, and she touched Angela's wrist where it was swollen. *We've waited long enough.* Angela leaned back in her chair. Look how small her hands were, her mother's hands with their bent fingers. She talked about alternative therapies, about a tree in Costa Rica with medicinal qualities in its bark, about Chinese herbs that stimulated the liver. There were mysteries in the world the doctors didn't know, and Angela said *yes, yes, you're probably right,* and her mother held her wrist. Her fingers left marks, indentations like dimples that took hours to fade.

They'd taken peginterferon together three times a week. Peginterferon via subcutaneous injection and ribivarin pills because the combination worked in fifty percent of people. They soaked the sheets with their sweat. They shivered and nothing warmed them and they were burning from inside. Forty-eight weeks of treatment and they lay together in bed unable to wash themselves or change the TV channel. Forty-eight weeks sicker than they'd ever been and none of it helped and none of it mattered and it felt so good to stop.

Thanksgiving weekend they went together to see her father. It was time to change his flowers. The sun had no mercy, her mother always said. Even in winter it faded their colors. Angela wore her coat in the car. They drove out past the old high school and the Citadel Mall where she'd spent every Friday with her friends, and she'd stolen a radio there once. She'd walked right through the doors. Past the city park and those red rocks in the distance where the Indians saw spirits. Clouds were blowing in from the mountains. She shielded her eyes from the blue of the sky. Things were beautiful, and she hadn't known. She'd thought only of leaving when she was young. She'd marked off the days until graduation because the coast was waiting. She'd follow the sun west and watch it set over the water, and all she'd done was trade one sort of beauty for another.

Her mother patted the headstone the way she used to brush his jacket. She was smoothing down his shoulders and whispering in his ear. She was someplace else, and Angela watched her from the car. She didn't want to walk that cemetery path. She never got out, not even in high school when her father was freshly buried. The markers made her uneasy, and his section used to be so empty and now it was almost full. There were soldiers buried there who'd died in Vietnam and in the Gulf, and they looked so young in their pictures. Earnest and sweet-cheeked as high school boys. Her mother set silk poinsettias in the pots on either side of the stone. She arranged them, and her scarf blew around in the wind. It wasn't like the graveyards in Europe. She'd said this many times. People didn't tend to their dead. The city didn't let the families grow roses or plant tulips for the spring, and the silk flowers were pretty but they weren't the same. Graveyards need something living and not just plastic and silk.

The car was getting cold. Angela rubbed her hands together and looked along the rows. Other cars were driving through. People were bringing pinwheels and fresh flags, and one lady had a plastic Santa Claus sitting in a sleigh. They decorated the graves and swept the snow off the stones, and she should have visited Gary more often. She should be more like her mother and set flowers on his grave.

They'd been sick together for three years. He'd stopped working first and then she stopped, too, and they stayed inside the apartment. They watched *Baywatch* reruns and old cartoons and anything but the news or medical shows. They shared their medicine and their needles, and none of it mattered. A hundred people had come to his memorial. They came from the studio and from his writers group, and his fraternity brothers came all the way from Ohio. Everyone came, it seemed like, everyone but her mother, and they waited in line to step up to the podium. They told stories about somebody she didn't know. She'd lived with him for almost ten years without ever learning he could juggle or that he'd played chess in high school. His brother told how Gary had stolen a scooter once from the college faculty lot. He drove it down the town hall steps and landed in the fountain. People laughed at that. They clapped their hands and shook their heads, and their stories made her lonely. Everything he'd seen and done, he took it with him. She'd already forgotten the sound of his voice.

Her mother stomped her boots before climbing back in. *Next time you'll come out,* she said. She drove slowly to the gate. She always drove slowly, even on Powers where the traffic was heavy and people were rushing to make the light. *You can't see the flowers from the car. You can't even read his name.* She turned on the defrosters because the windows were all steamed. They went past the matching stone benches where the city founders were buried. The Madonna stood between them, and her arms were open wide.

They walked the block at three o'clock most afternoons, and then they watched *Judge Judy.* Angela shuffled along. Even on cold days it was better than staying inside. The mantel clock made her nervous how it chimed every quarter hour. They were coming around on Brentwood when her right leg buckled. She felt no pain as she went down. She landed in a mound of freshly shoveled snow. It was soft as powder and not gray yet from the cars. Not like that Sierra snow that came down like cement. She lay on her back with her mother leaning over her. *What's wrong with your leg,* her mother was saying. *Did you slip on a patch of ice?* But Angela just lay there and looked up at the sky and her mother's worried face. She wasn't cold, and she wasn't frightened. She wanted only to lie back against the snow, to close her eyes and sleep.

Her mother brought out the wheelchair the first week in December, the foldable one from when she'd sprained her ankle in Boulder. It hurt worse than a fracture, her mother had said at the time. Sometimes it's better when things break clean. She took out the chair and wiped it down, and Angela didn't complain. What use was it when anyone could see that she couldn't walk, not even to the mailbox out by the fence. They went together around the block when the weather was clear because it was better than medicine to breathe in the air. Her mother talked while she pushed the chair. "What a shame about the Gerbers," she said. "They've really let things go. Every Sunday they go to Red Lobster but they've got no money for ice salt to keep folks from slipping." Angela nodded while her mother talked. She held tight to the armrests.

The neighborhood had changed. Her mother was right about that. The Danzigs were gone and the Lucas boys, too, and not even the snow could hide how the new folks had neglected their yards. And still Angela recognized those houses and the bare elm trees. Her mother struggled a little where the Cleyman's maple had cracked the cement. She pushed hard on the chair, and together they went over the sidewalk where Angela used to ride her bike. More than thirty years later and Angela knew it better than the streets she walked every day back in LA. She knew its cracks and how it curved and all the spots she'd fallen.

Five houses up another pair was approaching. A figure with someone else in a chair. As they came closer Angela recognized old Mrs. Needleman wrapped in a plaid blanket. Her granddaughter was pushing her along. "Look how nice they've got her covered," her mother said. "Last March she was a hundred. They showed her picture on *Good Morning America*. The Governor sent her a card."

Her mother waited in the Meyer driveway when Mrs. Needleman came close. "The sidewalk's too narrow for us both," she said in greeting. "Even when it's shoveled."

"Another day like this and the last of it will melt," the granddaughter said. She stopped the chair and stood on the sidewalk and looked up and down the street. "It's warm as April today."

"How are you, Mrs. Needleman?" Her mother reached for the old lady's hand. "It's a nice day for a walk."

Mrs. Needleman looked at Angela and at her mother and back at Angela again. "I remember you," she said. "You always walk that little dog and never pick up the poop." Her eyes were sharp. "You listen to that strange music."

"Mrs. Needleman," her mother said. "Angela hasn't been here in years. Not even to visit. She's been in Los Angeles. She decorates sets for movies."

"I want to go home," the old woman said. "I've got people waiting. My husband's waiting for me on the bridge."

The granddaughter shrugged as if to apologize. She held out both her hands and smiled. She's stopped making sense, she seemed to say, but Angela understood.

•

Starlings flew in formation just outside her window. At ten thirty every morning they went over the house and back again, and the sky was black with their passing. They moved as if pulled by some hidden current, and she leaned against the window frame to see. She wanted to take a picture of them. She wanted to capture them just as they were. She had the camera ready. She steadied her hands as best she could, but the pictures were unfocused and smudged by the screen. She just watched them after that. She leaned close to the window-sill, and her breath steamed against the glass. They should be some-place warmer, but they went over the treetops. Toward the mountains and back and around again, and she tried to remember them as they went. She tried to remember the sky and the snow on the peaks and those black winter birds. She wanted to take them with her.

Dialysis with the angry nurse who rimmed her eyes in liner. She wasn't gentle with the line. Dialysis until the dialysis would stop working. This is how it would go. One thing fails and then another and another one after that and the sky outside the window was beautiful as any she'd ever seen. A blue so pure it would burn your eyes and the wind lifted the snow from the rooftops and bent the naked branches.

We're just leaves on a tree. That's what Gary told her once. They were rockhounding in the Mojave. Looking for crystals in the trail-ings of old borax mines and the hills were pink in the distance. *Leaves on a tree,* and their hike wasn't even half done yet, and he closed his eyes the way he did when he was happy.

Sleep all day. Sleep from noon into night and then lie awake and lis-ten to the heater fire up in the basement. Listen to the wind as it blows. Sleep and more sleep and it was never enough. It was sweeter than food. Sweet as liquor and she wanted more. She slept when her mother pulled open the drapes. She slept when the vacuum cleaner ran or the doorbell chimed. She slept when her mother read from the book, and she didn't dream. No, she slept the way babies do. Like someone waiting to be born.

•

Once there was a boy who wanted only to go home. His boss wished him well and gave him a lump of gold as big as his head to thank him for his service. But the gold was heavy and when a rider came along the road, the boy gladly traded it for the horse. But the horse galloped and threw the boy and when a man came by with a cow, the boy traded in his horse because walking was better than riding. And the cow became a piglet because beef was stringy but the piglet had sweet juices. And the piglet became a goose because there was nothing better than crackling goose skin and the fat beneath. The boy was happy with all his trades until he saw a scissor-sharpener working by the road. *How lucky you are,* the boy said, *to know a fine craft.* The kind man looked around for a good sharpening stone and found one in the field. *Here you are,* he said, and the boy took the stone in exchange for his goose, and he was happy again because fate provided. But the stone was heavy and he wasn't careful and it fell into a stream. And the boy thought how lucky he was, how truly lucky, to be free of this heavy stone, and he walked the rest of the way home.

Things were crawling under her skin. They lived inside her belly. The slightest touch raised bruises. They spread in clusters across her legs, and on Christmas Eve the whites of her eyes turned yellow. She scratched her arms and her neck until her mother threatened to put mittens on her hands. "Those cuts will get infected," she said. "There's nothing wrong with your skin," but Angela scratched anyway. She tried to find those things that turned circles inside her. She needed to get them out, but they were always faster.

Her mother washed her in the tub. She sponged water over her head, and it was peaceful in the house. The clock was chiming and the windows were dark, and her mother turned the spigot because the water was getting cold. "All these things will wash away," she said. "You're the same as when you left."

She combed through Angela's hair and braided it loosely down her back. She talked, and Angela followed the sound of her words. She listened to their familiar rhythm. Her mother was saying it was the devil's virus. The devil should take it back. She needed to be strong for another day and another and the doctors would know what to do. Her eyes were black in the bathroom light. Dark like her mother's had been and like Angela's, too. And if Angela had had a daughter her eyes would have been dark, too, and it was a ribbon running through them, this blackness. It bound them all together.

"I'm sorry," her mother said. "I should have gone to his service. It wasn't right to stay away." She held Angela's hand like a parishioner looking for a benediction. She held it and squeezed it and cried.

It was time to ride in the car. She knew it without her mother saying so. Her mother didn't struggle when she lifted her up. How could that be? She was almost seventy, and she carried Angela from the wheelchair to the car. Her mother let the engine warm up and turned on all the heaters. She tucked a blanket around Angela and pressed her palm against her cheek.

They were going to the hospital. They were going to the high school and the cemetery and the Citadel Mall. The radio was playing, but Angela didn't know the song. It was one of her mother's stations. Her mother was talking. She was saying something. She was reading from the yellow book of stories, and Angela was lying in bed and she knew all the words. Hans im Glück was going home. He was free of all his gold. The stepmother chased the princes from their castle, and they were swans when they flew. They were starlings, and the sky was full with them.